Hill House Manor

13

Ghost Stories

Linda Anthony Hill

ISBN-13:978-1-7330814-3-6

Hill House Publishing

HillHousePublishing.com

Hill House Manor: 13 Ghost Stories is printed in Palatino Linotype, 12

Inspiration

These stories have all been inspired, in one way or another, by the infamous Hill House Manor in Gainesville, TX. Most of the names have been changed. The incident in Elizabeth, Sleep actually occurred in 198?. Many stories are inspired by individuals discovered during paranormal investigations at the house. Other characters are complete fiction. Linda often writes using Hill House Manor as a location in her mind's eye. Some people believe that a few of the stories are "channeled." They feel true, so who knows.

Some of the investigation scenes actually happened, like the one in the Lipan Apache Tribe. Some are a compilation of investigations that Linda has witnessed. Most of the spirits have been found from time to time over the years. If you like these stories, let Linda know. She loves writing them.

The Stranger

"This is my favorite spot for this time of day," said the older gentleman who seemed to have appeared out of nowhere. "The sun is barely down. The breeze is gentle, and the smell of honeysuckle scents the air ever so lightly."

"I didn't notice you come up," said Elise. "I must have been lost in thought. Is anyone else here yet?"

"Not that I know of," he said. "Are you expecting anyone?

"You're here for the hunt tonight, right?" she said. "I wasn't expecting anyone for another half hour. But I'm used to people arriving early."

"I'm just here for the porch," he said. "It's always so inviting."

It was an inviting porch, big enough for two rockers, a bench, and three chairs. At some point tonight it would probably be full of smokers. The front porch was the smoking section for the house. Non-smokers were welcome, but there was always someone out here smoking during these investigations.

The porch was covered and protected on three sides, making it perfect for visiting regardless of the weather.

"I'm sure there will be others arriving soo....," She stopped midsentence. He was gone. She had only looked away for a second if that. There was no sign of him.

"I guess tonight will be active," she said out loud as she continued waiting for the night's ghost hunters.

Table Of Contents

Story 1

The Early Years

In the beginning…

Albert was eager for the day to begin. It was going to be a long hard day, but in the end, his house would be more than doubled. He had already increased his ranch twice over by purchasing the Widow Scott's property. Now he would be moving that one-room house to join with his slightly smaller one-room home.

Albert's wife Mary had died of pneumonia. The loss of her children, who had been killed in an Indian raid, had been too much for her. She didn't even put up a fight when the pneumonia came for her. Soon after, Albert had set about finding another wife. The problem being that there were no eligible women out here on the frontier. So he had taken to looking in magazines in the classifieds. Some people called these women "mail order brides," but it wasn't as easy as that.

You had to find one to write to and then actually write letters to her to find out if she was what you were looking for. The first three Albert had written to had turned out to be city types that couldn't raise a potato or kill a chicken. He needed a woman who could keep the land and the house and survive while he was gone for days at a time.

He'd been writing with this fourth one for months, and she seemed like a good fit. Her looks were not that important to him, but she had sent a photograph and appeared to be a woman that was fair to look at. He only hoped she wasn't so pretty that passers-through would get ideas about her. That wouldn't do at all.

She had recently expressed a willingness to travel out to his homestead and to marry as early as it could be arranged. He was in bad need of help in the place, so this pleased him. Albert was not known to smile, but lately, he had at least grinned more than a few times.

Funny thing, after he had asked Gladys to join him with the intentions of matrimony, the widow Scott had decided that she could no longer maintain her late husband's homestead. She was returning to family in Arkansas and was selling as much as she could before the move. They had lived on a property adjoining Albert, and he regretted her leaving. He had hoped she would be there to be a friend to Gladys.

But he could not pass up this opportunity. He offered to buy her house if he could get enough help from other homesteaders to move it to his place and add it to his existing one-room home. This might be the first two-room house in the territory! He had ended up buying the property, and everything left on it, including the cattle.

Today was house moving day. The work had actually started days ago. The house he lived in had to be prepared to receive the new house. Foundation had to be laid. The widow's house had to be prepared. A path had to be created broad enough to allow the house to pass through the woods and over the creek. Today they would begin to move the house. With any luck, they would have it in place by tomorrow, and then he could start tying the two together.

This was important to have finished before Gladys arrived. He wanted her to have all the comforts of a sweet home. The water well was reasonably new. It was an added bonus and saved a lot of walking to the creek to fetch water.

The first day was the hardest. They had attached the long beams under the house and managed with an excellent team of horses to lift it off its foundation. That was the tricky part. Once it was free of the foundation, the moving began. They had made it all the way to the edge of Albert's ranch when they lost daylight, and everyone agreed to rest the horses and men for the night and resume in the morning.

The following day they moved the house into place and fixed it to the foundation. They joined the two rooms together at their respective back doors. It was precisely what Albert had envisioned. The widow had even left two chairs and a chest of drawers. One drawer was filled with personal items from the widow's late husband, Mr. Scott.

What caught his eye first was a deluxe whip that Albert had seen Mr. Scott put to good use on many occasions. (not all involving livestock, mind you.) He picked it up and felt the smooth worn handle fitting his hand like it had been made for him. There was a fine hand-carved comb, a shaving mug and razor, and a belt. Under two lovely handkerchiefs was a pistol whose wood grain glistened like glass. The gun looked almost new, but he had never seen a handle shine so. He laid his own sidearm in the drawer and put this treasure in its place at his side. He would be hard put to ever part with such a fine weapon. There were a whittling knife and a hunting knife with a handsomely carved handle. There was also a jug of whiskey.

He stood in his two-room house setting on what was now over Twelve-hundred acres, feeling like the wealthiest man on earth. And when his new bride arrived in a few days, he would also be the luckiest man on earth. Life was about to be better than it had ever been. He watched the sunset with a sense of pride.

Gladys was to arrive at the Trading Post. It was only half a day's ride from the house, but he would be pulling a wagon, so he needed to allow for a full day there. Dates were not always specific for these journeys, so Albert went in a day ahead to be sure to be there when she arrived. He took the wagon so there would be room for her things and anything she needed to pick up from the Trading post. He would pick up flour and salt and coffee and whatever else was available before she arrived. The Trading Post was handy, but they didn't stock much. Most things had to be ordered from a catalog.

The stage came in on the day it was supposed to, and Gladys was on it. She didn't look much like her picture, but it had been a long trip, and they had encountered Indians. They had lost one passenger, and the others were pretty shook-up, including Gladys. She had not counted on being so close to the Indian Territory, and she did not feel compelled to stay.

She wanted nothing but to rest up in whatever accommodations she could find at the Outpost and then get back to Ohio via Mississippi. She would not hear of going back the same way she had come, and she did not want to discuss it. Mr. Albert Dixon had not conveyed to her how dangerous the territory was nor how close they would be to the Indian Territory. She would not even speak to him.

He came to her the next day, thinking that a good night's rest might find her in better humor, but it did not. She was more determined to get back to civilization by way of the safest route possible, even if that meant spending extra weeks on the road. By the third day, she had found someone willing to escort her to the Mississippi River, and she made plans to remain for a few days and then leave on a more southeasterly path.

Albert was mad as a hornet. He had paid for her ticket out here, and he meant to have a wife. He had more than doubled the size of his home, he had used considerable time and resources preparing for a wife, and because of that, he had let the Widow Scott leave without trying to court her. All because Gladys was on her way. Now Gladys would be gone, and he would have to start over. To hell with luck! He wanted a wife!

After stewing for at least an hour, he decided to check at the Trading Post to see if they had a new magazine so he could begin his search again.

The Outpost was getting to be a busy place these days. Albert found out that there was a new town growing up around it. It was small, but it had some luxuries. There was, of course, a blacksmith, but there was also a small hotel with a restaurant. He had just been sleeping under a tree, but he was curious about the restaurant. He went in and sat down at one of two bench style tables. They were serving stew and cornbread, so he ordered some. It was good to eat something different from what he usually fixed himself. He felt his hand on his "new" gun and again started to feel like the wealthiest man alive.

He opened his new magazine to the personals and began to search. Here was one from

Tennessee. She would be more adaptable to this frontier life than those from farther back east. She had two sons. Hmmm. That would make for good hands around the place. How old were they? Nine and eleven. That would be perfect. Old enough to help, young enough not to cause trouble. Albert would have to pay for three tickets, but it would be worth it. And he had plenty of room now. This could be better than Gladys. He asked the hotel keep if he had some paper and a pencil. He needed to write this woman now.

No subtle dilly-dallying either. Albert would ask her straight up if she was ready to move and get married. She would have to sign a contract agreeing to be married the day she arrived, or he wouldn't pay for anything. He described himself and his homestead and his two-room house with a water well. That should impress her fair enough.

He took the letter to the Trading Post to get it sent out with the next mail run and headed back home.   Gladys was leaving and good riddance. It wouldn't have worked out if she was that faint-hearted anyway. This was harsh land, and it called for sturdy folk to claim it. It was better to find out now than a few months down the road. He made camp about half-way home. He should have camped by the Post and waited until morning to leave. This was not a safe territory to be camped alone, but he hadn't been thinking about a full day's ride hauling a wagon. He'd have been home before dark if he'd been on horseback.

Nothing for it now. He'd keep the fire low and sleep with one eye open. He was anxious, now, to be home. He'd been away too long. There was a cow needed milking and more chores than he cared to think about. He fell asleep thinking about his new bride to be. It was going to be excellent. Her name was Olivia. He liked it. It felt good on his tongue.

Albert awoke to the sound of the horse neighing. It was just before dawn, and the fire had died down to only a few embers. Something had spooked the horse, but he didn't see anything. Maybe just a snake, headed home from the night's hunt. He got up, put some twigs on the embers, and brought them back to life. He had some fresh coffee on the wagon and some salt-cured ham for breakfast. Once again, he felt like a king.

He was still half a day out from the homestead, and he didn't want to push it, so he finished up the coffee and climbed up on the wagon. The ride in was somewhat dull, which is preferable to getting attacked by Indians any day. He let the horse do most of the driving, and he just daydreamed a little more about how good life was going to be with

Miss Olivia in it. This was going to work out. He knew it.

As he approached the house, he realized that something was wrong. First off, there was smoke coming from the chimney. That couldn't be. He hadn't been there for days. Second, there wasn't a hen in sight. Were they hiding? Or were they gone?

He grabbed his rifle and checked his sidearm. He approached the house cautiously. When he was to the door, he called out. There was no answer. Could be someone was hiding in there. Could be they had already come and gone. There was only one way to find out. He kicked open the door with rifle cocked. There was no one in the first room. He moved further in and saw someone walk in the second room.

"Come on out!" he called.

There was no response.

"I said to come on out and show yourself!" he yelled a little louder.

Still no response. Albert walked entirely into the room. There was no one there. Had his eyes been playing tricks on him? He looked at the fireplace. It was cold. There hadn't been a fire there since he left. He felt a chill run down his spine. He'd heard of men losing their minds on the frontier. It was supposedly from being alone so much, but he had just been into the Trading Post. Hadn't he only been around people in the last few days? He couldn't be losing his mind. There had to be an explanation.

He turned to go back outside to bring in the supplies. He stopped abruptly. He had not taken anything from that drawer except the pistol. He thought about it, and he was sure. Yet, there on the wall by the door was the whip hanging on a nail. It was the perfect place for it. But he hadn't put it there. At least he didn't think he had. Had someone been in his house? Why would they leave such a beautiful whip on the wall instead of taking it? Curious.

He must have done it without thinking about it. That would explain why he didn't remember it. He shook his head as if to clear the cobwebs and reached for the door. He went out to the wagon and unhitched the horse, picked up the supplies that he had purchased in anticipation of having a wife with him, and brought them inside. It took a couple of trips. He looked at that whip every time he went out the door.

He went out to look for the chickens. What he found was a lot of feathers. He suspected that the coyotes had paid a visit. As he approached the remains, he heard a faint clucking coming from a distance. He walked up the hill a bit and found two hens hiding under a bush, and above them in a tree was the rooster. At least he wasn't cleaned out. This was plenty enough to make a fresh start, and he wouldn't need too many eggs until he had a woman around. Strange how those birds stayed safe. And just enough to start over. He guessed he was still pretty lucky.

As the days went by, Albert worked on the house. He had the walls and doorways all fixed so that it seemed the houses had always been one house. He built a cupboard near the fireplace, then moved it into the second room. His future wife could make the final decision of where she wanted it.

He built a nice coup for the chickens to keep them safe from coyotes and such. They seemed to like it. There were chicks now, and he knew that soon enough, they would be hens. There would be enough for eggs and plenty for Sunday dinners.

Some strange things were happening in the add-on room that he couldn't explain. It made him feel forgetful as he would leave and come back, and things wouldn't always be where he left them. It was a worrisome thing to happen even once, but it was frequently happening. Sometimes he would pretend that he had forgotten that he had moved them in the first place, but that was getting harder and harder to do. Things from the second room would usually end up in the original house like they were returning home.

Albert would go to the Outpost every week to check for mail. They told him they would deliver anything that came in for him on the regular two-week run, but he went in anyway, "just to check." He also kept looking at the new classifieds. He hadn't seen anyone who would measure up to Olivia.

One day a rider came in, a postman. He had gotten a response. Olivia was happy to accept his offer and would be arriving in a week's time. She had bought her own tickets. A week's time? What date had this been sent? It had been almost a week ago. She would be at the Outpost any day. He asked the postman if he wanted to come in and have some coffee. It was the polite thing to do. Even offered to let him spend the night, but it was early in the day yet, and he had another ranch to visit. Albert was glad of it. He didn't want to seem impolite, but he needed to get to the Post.

Albert hitched up the wagon and took off as soon as the postal rider was out of sight. It wouldn't do for Miss Olivia to have to wait on him.

They didn't have a contract. No sense losing her to anyone who happened to be in that new little town. He didn't even stop to put on Sunday clothes. He just took off.

It was past dark when he arrived at the Trading Post. He checked with the Postmaster to see if she had already come. Not yet. His luck was holding. He made camp under a tree and slept until dawn. He went over to the Trading Post to wait. The clerk told him it would be early afternoon before the stage arrived. He looked around and spotted some ribbon that would make a fitting welcome gift for Olivia. He had them wrap it extra special for her. He was pretty proud to have thought of it. He went off to see if there was anything new in town.

He walked over to the blacksmith and had a long conversation with Mr. Smith. He didn't get to visit with folks too often, and it felt good. It made him feel more civilized. He talked with him about designing a branding iron for him. They spoke about a lazy D. Mr. Smith said he would start working on it. And Albert noted mentally that nothing was moving on its own around here either.

He heard dogs barking and realized the stage was arriving. He scurried out and walked as swiftly as he could without running in the direction of the stage landing. Albert stood there, waiting for the passengers to come down. There were several trunks on the top of the coach, and he wondered if they all belonged to Olivia. He might have to build some more dressers or even a closet.

The woman who appeared at the coach door was healthy-looking. She had plenty of meat on her bones, and he could tell that she had worked a farm or a ranch. And from the looks of her, she could cook. She wasn't beautiful, but she wasn't hard to look at either. He was excited to meet her and rushed up to her to help her down. She let him know right away that she was here for someone in particular, and he shouldn't go getting any ideas. He liked that. He told her his name, and her face softened. He handed her the package with the ribbon in it. She blushed a little.

She had not expected him to be there to greet her. She had thought that she might have to get a room for at least one night. But here he was and not unpleasant to look on either. She smiled.

Her sons pushed their way through, and the older one offered his hand. "I'm Tom," he said. "Where should I put my mother's trunks?"

"Load 'em up in the wagon, boy," said Albert to the scrappy youngster.

"Mr. Dixon, you spoke of marriage, and I think we should take care of that before we do anything else. Is there a Justice of the Peace that can help us with this?" Her voice was crisp with a flute-like quality. It was not the harsh sound he was expecting. This was like a dream coming true.

"I've made all the arrangements (the papers were leftover from Gladys, so all they had to do was change the name and date. The license would still work.) I have a license, and there is a preacher at the Post right now who can do the joinin'."

"It's a pleasure to find a man who knows how to get a job done," Olivia cooed.

"Should I get you a room for the night, so you can rest before the ceremony and before the journey to the homestead?" he offered.

"I should like to get the marrying taken care of first if you don't mind. I will feel much more secure when I am Mrs. Dixon."

Albert gave a local boy a nickel to see to the wagon and led Miss Olivia and sons to the Trading Post. They were married in a matter of minutes by the preacher that Albert had mentioned. Folks in the territory had need of a Preacher from time to time, and he also held the title Justice of the Peace.

Albert and Olivia both seemed to be no-nonsense kinds of people. It already seemed like a perfect match.

"Does our house have a bed?" Olivia asked.

"I have a feather mattress on the floor, Miss Olivia."

"We." She said.

"What?"

"We have a feather mattress on the floor. We will be partners in everything or nothing," said Olivia sweetly.

"Of course," said Albert. "I wouldn't have it any other way." He liked how she spoke her mind. " It's more than a day's drive to the ranch. Do you want to rest up here in town overnight?" he asked.

She looked at the sun and realized they only had a couple of hours of daylight left. They wouldn't make it very far before having to make camp for the night. It was a good idea to sleep in a bed one last time.

"Yes, let's spend the night here and then leave bright and early."

"I'll get you and the boys a room," he said. "I'll make camp out in the woods."

"Nonsense!" said Olivia. "You will do no such thing. You will sleep with your wife tonight. I won't hear of having it any other way."

With that settled, they headed for the hotel and found that for an extra quarter, they could get a room with a side room for the boys. They would have a little privacy for their honeymoon night. There was also a bath next door to the hotel. So he could get cleaned up. This was getting better and better.

The boys wanted to go explore the Outpost, and Albert saw no harm in it, so they ran off to see if they could find any real soldiers and with luck, other boys their age. For the first time, Albert and Olivia were alone together.

"You're a fine lookin' woman, Miss Olivia," said Albert. He wasn't very experienced at courting or wooing a woman. He didn't even have a lot of practice talking to them.

"Please call me Olivia or Liv or Livvy would be nice," She said almost shyly.

"Alright, Miss Livvy," he stammered a little.

"Livvy will do," she said.

"I don't have a lot of experience bein' 'round folk," he spurted out. "I spend most of my time alone. Don't like it none, but it's what I do, and it's part of livin' in this territory. There's more people comin', but they ain't here yet. It's a lonely life you're choosin'. You sure you want this?"

"Yes, I'm sure." She snuggled up to him and put her head on his shoulder. She stroked his cheek with her hand. They spent a little time getting to know each other in the biblical sense.

When they were finished "getting to know each other," they decided to check out the Bathhouse next door. Albert let her go first, then he used the same water to save a nickel. She hadn't been all that dirty anyways, and they were definitely going to have to dump it when he was through. He thought about getting a fancy tub for their own place. Livvy would probably like that. He had always just gone down to the creek when he got to feeling too dirty. Which wasn't all that often. Livvy deserved a tub. He would check at the Trading Post before they left and see how much it would cost to order one. He would start putting the money back right away.

He was thinking of all the things he wanted to build on the property and add to the house. It was exciting to have a woman who would be willing to

19

pitch in and help and boys who seemed capable of doing their share of chores. He could hardly wait to get back home and get started.

The boys wandered back in, and they all walked over to the stage office to see about a meal. They had beans and bread. Standard fare. It was enough. They ate and went back to the hotel.

He had forgotten how nice it was to sleep with a woman. They snuggled off and on during the night and even "got to know" each other a few more times. She was an amazing woman, and he couldn't believe his good fortune to have found her.

They woke up before dawn. There was a troop of soldiers camped near the Outpost, and Reveille was hard to sleep through. Olivia had the boys get ready, and they went downstairs for a bit of breakfast before the long drive home. Albert was shocked at how much it costs to feed four. He was still happy to have them all and thought the first job should be to make an off the floor bed for Olivia and himself. Then he could make some bunks for the boys. They could, of course, help him with all of this. Yes, this was going to be very good.

They climbed aboard the wagon and started to head out. The horse was weighed down by all the passengers and trunks. Albert wished he had brought Paint (his riding horse) along. Maybe he should look at a horse while here. It wouldn't hurt to have three now with this instant family. He went over to the stable to see if the Blacksmith knew of anyone looking to sell a good horse at a fair price. Mr. Smith happened to know someone and directed Albert to him. Albert had Olivia and the boys wait in the wagon for him. In fifteen minutes, he was back with a horse and bridle. This time when they set out, they were moving at a pretty good clip. Not as fast as a stagecoach, but fast enough to get home by dark.

Albert and Olivia talked a lot on the trip. He told her about the ranch, and she told him about where she had come from and what she could do around the place. Turned out, she had ideas for the family garden and was thinking they would run cattle. She was an ambitious woman and not afraid of hard work. He told her about the Indian raids, and she said she was a fair shot with a rifle and had one of her own in her trunk. Albert felt, once again, like the king of the world.

They stopped to rest and have some bread they had brought from the restaurant. The boys took off exploring, and they had to be told not to go too far. There could be Indians. The Indian Territory was across the Red River, and it dipped pretty far into Texas near Albert's homestead. The Indians had been somewhat quiet the last few months, but you never knew what they were thinking. They raided and killed for the pleasure of it sometimes. The boys would have to learn to shoot.

"They know how to shoot," said Olivia. "They have their own rifles in the same trunk as mine."

"Bless my soul," said Albert. "You could do this on your own without a man, couldn't you?"

"Might could," she said. "But it wouldn't be near as much fun, and I know it would be more difficult. I like having a man around to protect me."

"Seems to me you are pretty good at protecting yourself," he said. He couldn't hide his disappointment at not being as necessary as he wanted to be.

"A woman has to learn to be when she's raising two boys alone," she said. "But I want nothing more than to go back to being a wife and mother. Never forget that my boys and I will always have your back."

As if on cue, the boys came running up to the wagon yelling, " Indians! Indians!"

Just then, an arrow hit the wagon. "which trunk?" yelled Albert.

"The one on top!" yelled Olivia.

He tossed her his rifle and yelled, "Cover me!"

He lept to the side of the wagon and opened the trunk just in time to stop an arrow with the lid. He grabbed the rifles, left the cover open, and rejoined his new family.

"Are they loaded?" he said.

"Yep," she replied.

The boys grabbed their guns and sat waiting. They knew not to fire until there was something to fire at. An Indian came running from the woods, and Albert shot him dead. Two more came running, and two more went down. Had Albert been alone, he would probably have had a much more difficult fight on his hands. Reloading would have given the enemy time to be upon him.

"How many did you see, boys?" Albert asked.

"Maybe five," the oldest boy answered.

"Stay sharp. Them other two are still out there. Y'all climb into the wagon and stay low. I'm gonna' steer us outa' here before they shoot one of the horses."

Albert ducked low and drove the wagon west and a little south and away from the woods. They were still hours from the house, and he definitely wanted to be there by nightfall now. "Did you see any horses, or were they on foot?" he asked the boys. Both boys agreed that they hadn't seen any horses. "Good, maybe we can leave them behind." He cracked his whip, and the horses sped up to a full gallop. He hated pushing them this hard, but everyone's lives were hanging in the balance, including the horses. They went for at least a mile before he let them slow down.

The ranch at the end of the trail was deeper into the frontier than the place the little group had been ambushed. They weren't traveling towards safety. But headed into even more dangerous territory. Albert stopped long enough for Olivia to rejoin him in the front of the wagon and the boys to get situated where they could each see one side and the rear. Their rifles were ready now. Olivia carried hers in her lap.

The farther they went, the better they felt. It may have been a small raiding party, and they had snuck up on the wrong family. The family stayed alert but began to relax a bit. The sun was an hour from setting when they pulled up to the house. The boys carried the trunks inside and went to get firewood. The older boy, Tom, drew water from the well, and the younger boy, Mark, helped his mother get the fire going.

Albert went out to check on the chickens and the milk cow. Everything was alright, and it didn't look like the Indians had paid them any visits in the two days he had been gone. Mark asked if he could feed the chickens, and Albert showed him where the feed was.

Olivia put together a quick meal and started making herself at home. She had brought some of her own pans and flatware, but she would need to come up with another plate. There were bowls and some cookware. She found some canned goods and flour and jerky. She could make do with this for a bit. She would have Mark collect eggs in the morning, and Tom could take over the milking.

The feather mattress looked plenty comfortable, and the boys would sleep on the floor by the fire. This was a good-sized house and more than she had expected considering where they were. Albert had done well, and she would help him turn this into a beautiful estate. She had heard on the stage that there was to be a Fort built a few miles south of Albert's place. Ft. Fitzhue they had called it. It should be constructed in the next few months. It would not be a big Fort, but it would mean soldiers nearby and help with the Indians.

This would prove to be a good move for her. She was sure of it. Now, where was that ladle she had just laid down by the fire? One of the kids must have picked it up. They better not lose it.

After their encounter with the Indians today, they were all a little hesitant to go to sleep. They felt like they were being watched, and decided to take turns standing watch, with Albert first. He sat, looking at his new family. They had fought well today and proved they could stick in this paradise with thorns. It was good land, and there was plenty of game and room for livestock, with woods, fields, and creeks, a real paradise. But those Indians were a mighty big thorn.

After a few hours, Albert felt himself dozing off. He woke Olivia and asked if she felt up to taking the watch for an hour or two. She got up and let him lie down. The night had been quiet so far, and the bed was surprisingly comfortable. She pulled out a book and began to read. There were a few times that the light from the fire played tricks on her eyes, and she thought she saw the shadow of a man on the wall near the door. She put the book down and moved to the window. She opened the shutter a crack so she could stare out at the property. It was a beautiful place and would be even better with four of them to tend to it. It was all so peaceful.

She woke with a start as Albert rested his hand on her shoulder. She apologized profusely for having fallen asleep. It was not like her to let her guard down like that. She was so, so sorry.

"It's okay," he whispered. "No harm done. I got all the sleep I needed, and it will be mornin' soon. Go get a little more sleep."

"I'll need to start the coffee and get some biscuits going," she said. She fussed around with the fire and started the coffee. She was glad Tom had brought in water the night before. Mark stirred and sat up.

"Mamma, is it time to get up?"

"Yes, dear. Sun will be breaking soon. Then you can go look for some eggs. Won't that be a nice breakfast?" she said.

"Is it safe to go out there, yet?" he asked.

"I don't reckon they'll be botherin' us today," said Albert. "We put up a good fight yesterday. They'll think twice about attacking the house."

"Then, I need to go to the outhouse," said Mark.

"I'll walk out there and keep an eye out for ya'" said Albert. "Then, I'll show you the hen coop."

27

Olivia looked down by the hearth, and her ladle was right where she had left it. How had she missed that? She must have looked right at it. Strange, very strange.

Tom woke up. He asked Olivia if she needed him to do anything. She told him to bring in some more wood. He went out and visited with Albert for a minute and then found the wood, brought in an armful, and laid it by the fire. He knew better than to add wood when mamma was cooking. She would take care of it and keep the fire precisely the way she wanted it for what she was cooking. He went back outside to explore the property in daylight.

Albert showed the boys around, and they started talking about chores. Mark would take care of the chickens and had already decided they needed a bigger house. He would get started on it after breakfast. Tom would take care of the as yet to be named milk cow, and the horses. He thought the horses needed a shelter and asked if he and Albert could work on one together. Albert was impressed with them both.

Olivia called them to breakfast. They hurried in, and Albert was impressed to find biscuits and jerky gravy and a couple of scrambled eggs.

"Tom," he called. "Come back in here and join us for some breakfast."

"I'm right here, Mr. Dixon," said Tom, who was standing behind him.

"Then who is in the other room?" asked Albert.

"No one," the boys said in unison.

"I saw someone move in there," Albert said.

He walked into the next room and looked all around. There was no one there. The trunks were in there and the feather bed and the dresser from the widow Smith. He lit a lamp and looked closer. He knew he had seen someone. But the room was empty. He went back into the main room for breakfast. His imagination was getting out of hand. He felt his face go to a frown.

The conversation was lively as everyone talked about their plans for the day. Albert announced that he would help, but his priority was to make a bed for himself and Olivia. The boys agreed that they would help with that first and then start on their own projects.

With breakfast finished, they cleared the table and headed out to begin the task of building a bed. Albert had some rough-hewn lumber set aside, and he picked through it for what they would need. The boys picked through what was left for their own projects. They only fought over a few pieces, and Albert put a stop to that with nothing but a sideways glance. Albert had a pretty mean face when he felt like it. The boys made note never to get on his bad side.

Olivia tidied up the house. She opened her first trunk and decided to put some of her things in the empty dresser drawers. There was room to transfer an entire trunk with one drawer left for the boys. Her next chest was kitchen items, and she dragged the trunk into the main room. She could work out of the chest until Albert was able to put up some shelves. She found her spices and yeast and felt relieved to be able to put together a decent meal for the evening. If the dough was started now, they would have bread by evening. It would have to be a round bread until she could talk Albert into a proper wood stove, but it would taste fine, and she would make do.

Albert came in to measure the feather mattress, and Olivia asked him about shelves.

"I made this cupboard for you. We just need to move it to where you want it," he said. "I'll take care of it right now."

She showed him where she wanted it, and he moved it three times before it was exactly right. She immediately began to fill it with spices and flatware and dishes and pans.

"It would be nice to have a cookstove," she said. "Maybe we can get a catalog?" she said as more of a question than a demand.

"I had that very thought," said Albert. "But I was thinkin' we'd look for a fancy bathtub." He winked as he said it. "We'll have to get some crops goin' to raise the money for it, though."

"or some cattle," she added.

"AND some cattle," he said emphatically. He hadn't told Olivia about the Scott's cattle, yet.

Albert went back out to continue building the bed. It wasn't going to be anything pretty but would do to get Olivia off the floor. It took two days to make it, and he assembled it right there in the room. He wasn't sure it would ever come out. It had four posters of rough-hewn pine and no footboard or headboard yet. Just a box with a mattress on it.

Olivia hugged him and thanked him and hugged him again. She was overjoyed, almost crying. It was simple, but to her, it was the most beautiful piece of furniture she would ever have.

The boys caught a rabbit while Albert was working on the bed. So, they had fire-roasted rabbit for dinner. It was a feast in a castle. They looked forward to going on a real hunt for deer meat soon. Albert promised they would.

The next day was spent on the boy's projects. Things were taking shape, and the little homestead was turning into a Ranch. Soon they would have to go into the blacksmith and get that branding iron. Then the fun would begin.

Within a few days, the "men" went on a hunt, leaving Olivia home alone. They didn't go very far until they found fresh tracks. They slipped quietly through the woods until they came upon a small clearing. There were two bucks, three does and a yearling. Albert took aim on the bigger buck. Before he could get off a shot, the deer fell. It had been taken down with an arrow.

The other deer scattered, and the hunter emerged cautiously from the wood. Then another joined him. They had almost infringed on a hunting party from what looked like the Chickasaw that had probably crossed the Red River following the deer. This was not their territory, but Albert wasn't going to try to stake any claims today. He and the boys kept very still. The Indians gathered up their kill and tied its feet up to a carrying pole. They disappeared back into the woods. Albert and the boys slipped off in the opposite direction.

They headed a little further south to put some distance between them and the Red River. They came across another set of tracks, and within an hour, they had their own deer ready to carry home. Olivia would be pleased.

They would eat well for a few days, and then they would begin drying and curing what was left. Life was good.

Albert was always on high alert now. Those Indians were only hunting, but it showed him that they had no respect for the Red River as a border. That was worrisome to him, and he cautioned the boys to stay on their guard and keep an eye on their mom when she was out.

That new Fort couldn't come too soon, but they were building it about four miles south of him. If they put it north of him, it would sure put him more at ease. But more activity in the area was great no matter where it was. The more people came, the more the Indians would shy away. It sounded good, anyway.

Time passed, and the chicks became hens producing enough eggs to have more than they needed. They had a nice fried chicken dinner, too. When the new Fort was built, they would have someone close to sell the eggs to. But they could also always take a few dozen in to exchange at the Trading Post. That was what they would do this week. In a few months, they might be going instead to Ft Fitzhugh.

Albert took Tom on horseback with him to the Trading post and picked up his branding iron. It was time to lay claim to the Scott's cattle and calves and round up his own cattle and brand them, too. The branding-iron was ready, and Mr. Smith gladly took a chicken and a dozen eggs in trade.

There was a small General Store opening up. Livvy would be happy for that. They went over to check it out. It wasn't open, but Mr. and Mrs. Potts were busy putting things up on the shelves. They stopped to talk and introduce themselves. They were happy to hear about Olivia. They gave Tom a piece of hard candy for him and one to take back to his brother. Albert noticed that they had fabric and canned goods, and more. He couldn't wait to bring Livvy in.

Albert and Tom headed back to the ranch with their branding iron and a few other items they had picked up. It was an uneventful trip, and that suited them fine. As they approached the house, they heard a gunshot and saw three riders hightail it out to the South. They sped up to the house to find Livvy standing on the porch with her rifle in hand.

"Albert! Albert! Thank heaven you're back!" she yelled as she saw Albert and Tom speeding to the porch.

"What happened?" they asked together.

"They was tryin' to rob us!" yelled Mark. "They tried to sneak up on us, but Mamma saw 'em comin'. She let 'em git almost to the door when she flung it open and yelled for 'em to stop right there."

"Albert, I never been so scared," cried Olivia. "I don't know what they wanted, but when they saw my rifle, they stopped. I fired once over their heads, and they lit out."

Just then, they saw the three riders approaching again. One of them had a white flag raised up over his head.

"Stop right there," yelled Albert.

They stopped. "Mister, we're Texas Rangers. Got the papers to prove it if you want to see. We're here to help."

"Livvy, keep that rifle on 'em. Tom, go get yours. Where's Mark?"

"He's inside the house," said Olivia.

"Mark, set your sight on the one on the left," said Albert

"Yes, sir," called Mark.

"One of ya' come on in slow. I'll look at yer papers," said Albert.

The one in the middle that was carrying the white flag got off his horse and walked in slowly. He obviously wasn't wanting to get shot today. "Here you go. They're all official and signed and stamped. We even got badges, see?" he pointed to his badge.

Albert looked at the paper and passed it to Olivia. She set her gun down and breathed a loud sigh of relief. "I am so sorry!" Olivia yelled out. "It was just my boy and me here, and we've had trouble with Indians, and a woman can't be too careful out there, and I wasn't expecting anybody to come riding up, and..." she was panting for breath now.

"Easy, Olivia," said Albert. "You don't have to apologize for defending yourself nor explain it, neither. Fellas, come on up. What can we do for ya'. Would you like some coffee?"

The Rangers came on up and introduced themselves. They were here looking to the building of the Fort. This was border country, and they were trying to get a feel for how many people were here and what kind of trouble they'd been having with the Natives.

Albert told them about the hunting party he and the boys had run across. He told them where they were at the time and then told them about the raid on him and his family, the day he had picked them up and brought them in.

"We see signs of them from time to time, but we try to avoid 'em when we can," he finished up.

"We'll try to swing this way every few weeks," the tall one said, "If you think you can keep your wife from shootin' at us." They all laughed.

There was some chit chat about the new fort and the trail east and all the new settlers they were expecting. Daylight slipped away before they knew it.

"Y'all are welcome to camp out back for the night, boys," said Albert. "It's not safe ridin' around here at night."

"Thank you, Mr. Dixon. We will."

Albert felt pretty safe with three Texas Rangers camped out in the back yard for the night. Olivia invited them for dinner, and they stayed up late swapping stories and catching up on news from Austin and hearing about the new fort. It turned out that it wasn't to be much more than a building and a couple of men, but that was more than they had now, so they were happy to have it. Even the boys stayed up. They had a lot of questions for real Texas Rangers.

Next morning Olivia woke to the sight of someone pouring coffee. She turned and saw that Albert was still in bed. She started to get up, and they were gone. It wasn't like they'd left. They disappeared. She decided it must have been one of the Rangers, and she must have had some sleep in her eyes and missed them walking out.

She got up and drew the curtain to change. After she was dressed, she went to get the fire going and then out to the outhouse. The rangers were all three still in their bedding. Who had been in the house? Why hadn't it woken the boys? Was she losing her mind?

As she walked back inside, the rooster started crowing, and everyone started stirring. She quickly forgot about what she had seen and soon, it was like it had been part of a waking dream. She made coffee and biscuits and gravy for everyone. The rangers came in and said they might be back sooner if all her cooking was this good. She blushed but accepted the compliment with grace.

After they left, she told Albert about her "dream." He told her about some of the things he had seen. Things like seeing someone in the next room when there was no one there and having things seem to vanish and then show up in the other room. She remembered her ladle and shared that with him. They decided not to tell the boys. But they promised to start telling each other whenever something strange happened.

Olivia started making entries in a diary. She had heard of places where strange things happened. Some said it was the spirits of those who had passed. But, they were on the frontier. Who could have died here? She made a mental note to ask Albert about that next time they were alone.

Later in the day, when the boys were busy with their projects, Olivia pulled Albert into the house and asked him who had died here.

"The boys were killed by Indians during a raid while I was out working a fence line. They were outside when the Indians attacked. The wife was too late to help them. They were out in the woods gathering kindling. By the time she knew what was happening, they were dead, and the raiders had made off with our workhorse. The wife was here in the main room when she died later that winter of pneumonia."

"Why was your wife in the main room? Why wasn't she in bed in the bedroom?" asked Olivia.

"This was only a one-room cabin until a few months before you got here, Livvy. The bedroom was the widow Scott's house. Me and some friends moved it over and joined it to my house."

"The widow? What happened to her husband?" asked Olivia.

"Indians got him. They left him for dead, but he made it back to their house. I reckon he died in this room here. 'cept it was a couple miles from here at the time," said Albert.

"Oh my," said Olivia. "That's a lot of spirits to be wandering about. We will need to call in a minister to bless the house and purge it of all these spirits. Will you take me to the Potts's store tomorrow to find out who can help?"

"People will think we're crazy, Livvy!" yelled Albert. "I don't think we need to be tellin' people we got spirits here."

"Well then, take me to the minister. I'll swear him to secrecy. He will have to help us. Don't you think?" Olivia was pleading.

Albert couldn't deny her anything, so he agreed. They would make a trip a couple of days **after** the cattle were rounded up and branded. That could take a few weeks, but it had waited this long, it could wait another month.

They could take the wagon, and the boys could visit with the Potts' boy. They'd need some supplies by then if there were any to be had. There were a few chickens to trade. They could take all three horses and make a little trip out of it. A month wasn't so long to wait.

In the mean-time, Olivia wrote a letter to her sister to try and find her a book on hauntings and blessings and getting rid of spirits. She sent her enough money to pay for the book and the postage. Of course, it would be a while before she saw a postman, but she felt better just having written the letter. She fell asleep that night thinking of all those souls that had died here. There was so much tragedy in these walls. Her eyes filled with tears for poor Albert, having lost so much.

The roundup went well. The boys caught on quickly and were more helpful than Albert had anticipated they would be. He had hired a hand to help, as well. Together they made short work of it, and the roping and branding went equally smooth. Each of the boys wanted to brand at least one calf, and Albert was proud to let them. He knew he worked them pretty hard, but they enjoyed so much of it that he didn't feel guilty about the rest.

They ended up with fifty new calves. This was a record, and they would be able to sell off a third of the herd. Albert saw a cookstove and a bathtub in their future. Livvy would be pleased.

Olivia had received a book from her sister and a small package of seeds. The seeds were for sage, which would be used in the ritual of reclaiming their house from the spirits. The book contained the prayers and procedures that she and Albert would need to use. There was also a small crystal that was to be cleansed in the stream under a full moon and then buried near the threshold of the house. She was thankful for the book. She would also look for a minister to bless the house, but these were things that she could do herself, and that made her feel easier.

She went out to the garden to plant the seeds. These were herb sage and wouldn't grow like a bush. She planted them in the herb garden. She wondered if Texas sage would work. It grew in several places on the ranch. She would have the boys gather her some. They could at least try it while they were waiting for the white sage to grow.

She took the crystal down to the stream and placed it in the water in a way that would keep it from being carried off by the stream. She would leave it there until tomorrow evening. She was beginning to feel much more hopeful about her future here.

Albert thought it was all a bit silly, but he didn't mention that to Olivia. He would do whatever she wanted him to if it would make her feel safer. She seemed more afraid of the spirits than she was of the Indians now.

It was time to make arrangements to sell some cattle, and he would be driving them East with the new hired hand and Tom. They would pick up another hand or two in the new town. He didn't want to leave Livvy and Mark alone, but it had to be done. The Rangers would look in on them from time to time, and the men at the new fort would do the same. They would be okay. He would stay long enough to "cleanse" the house of spirits for her. And see if it had worked.

They used the Texas sage that the boys had gathered. They said the prayer and walked all around the rooms with the burning sage. They followed the directions exactly. When they were finished, there was still some sage, so Olivia decided they could do the same on the outside of the house. Albert felt a little foolish, but he went along. He would be leaving tomorrow for what could be a long trip and wanted her to feel protected.

The next day the cattle drive began. It was a small herd, and they weren't driving them far. They would be selling them to another rancher who would herd them further East in a month or two along with a thousand more. Everyone said their goodbyes and Olivia's eyes filled with tears as she kissed her husband and her oldest son goodbye. She went into the house to cry alone. Mark came in a few minutes later to tell her they were gone and to reassure her that they would be okay.

By the end of the next day, a rider approached. It was a woman, though she was dressed more like a man.

"Mr. Dixon said he had enough help for the drive, but that you might be able to use a hand here," she said as she rode up. "I was really hopin' to help out with the drive. I can handle cattle as good as any man. I can also fence and rope and do what needs doin' around here. And it never hurts to have another gun out here. Can I stay?"

Olivia sighed in relief. She had not realized how nervous she was about being on the place alone for so long. Albert had known, and he had shown her how much he cared in that simple gesture. She would rest much easier now. She went in and made the girl a plate of dinner.

"What is your name, child," asked Olivia as she brought the plate to her.

"I ain't no child. My name is Charlotte, but I go by Charlie," she replied.

"Fair enough," said Olivia. "You may call me Olivia or Mrs. Dixon, whichever you prefer. I see you have a bedroll, and you may use it by the fireplace inside. Or my son's bunk bed is available until the men get back from the cattle drive."

"Thank you," said Charlie. "I'll take the bunk."

"We can talk about chores tomorrow," said Olivia. "There is a horse stable that needs tending and many other things that will need doing."

"I don't mind doing whatever needs to be done," replied Charlie.

Mark was speechless. He had never seen a girl dressed like a man, and he didn't know how to act. She was pretty in a way, and her eyes sparkled when she talked. He decided he liked her.

Olivia realized that nothing strange had happened around the place since she and Albert had "cleansed" it. She was most grateful for that hoping it would last, and wondering if they still needed the house blessed by a minister. She no sooner thought it than her hairbrush wasn't where she usually kept it. It was unsettling for many reasons. Were they reading her mind now? She went to look for it in the next room. Sure enough, there it was on the shelf by the fireplace.

She would not have put it there. She kept it on the dresser. She always kept it in the same place. No one had been in here, but she asked Charlie anyway. "Did you happen to borrow my hairbrush, Charlie?"

"No, Ma'am. I didn't," Charlie answered. "I have a comb in my saddlebag."

That answered the question she had been thinking. She still needed a minister. And maybe she needed the white sage that she was growing in the garden. Could it be Texas sage just wouldn't work? It was a bush, after all, not an herb. Could that make a difference? Olivia fought down the panic rising in her chest. The spirits never hurt anyone. They were pranksters, moving things about. And Albert had even guessed that they had been helpful on a couple of occasions. Like when the chickens were hidden from the coyotes. She calmed herself back down.

Olivia didn't tell Charlie about the spirits. No reason to scare her off. She felt better with the girl here. She had proven handy with a gun. They were eating venison this week because of her skills. And she was teaching Mark to use a bow. They had also made a lot of progress on the stable. Most of the horses were gone on the cattle drive, so it was easier to work on it.

Olivia would keep the hairbrush incident to herself and hope that the resident spirits didn't play any tricks on Charlie. Maybe she should dig up that crystal and put it in the stream again at the next full moon. She would do that and say a few more prayers.

The days passed quickly, and in another week, a new rider approached.

"Hello, I'm Reverend Handy. Your husband sent me to bless your home for you. He said you had concerns about those who had died here and wanted a proper blessing of the place."

Olivia was stunned. First, Albert had sent a ranch hand and now a minister. She was beginning to feel real love for this grizzly man and was never so happy to see anyone than she was to see this man of the cloth come to bless their home and rid them of any spirits that were playing tricks on her. She was too overwhelmed to speak to the man properly.

"I, I, I, I don't know what to say. I cannot thank you enough for coming. Please, come in, sit by the fire and rest yourself," she said.

"The truth is, I am a traveling minister, and this is the farthest west I have come. I didn't know we had any settlers this far west. I'm hoping you will join us in town for a revival next month. I'm spreading the word and hope to have a large crowd."

"What town?" asked Olivia.

"I don't even know if it has a name," said Reverend Handy. "It is near the Outpost East of here. The Potts general store is at the heart of it. I just call it Potts town."

"That's where we go for supplies," said Olivia. "I know the Potts'. They are good people. I do hope we can make it to your revival. Please, have a seat. Can I offer you some coffee?"

"That would be excellent," said Rev. Handy. "Then you can tell me about the spirits that seem to be bothering you."

Olivia brought Mr. Handy a cup of coffee and began to tell her story, "They don't actually bother me. They play tricks and hide things from me. I would really like to have the ranch blessed and maybe see the spirits put to rest."

"I can certainly bless the house and the ranch," said Rev. Handy. "It would be my pleasure to do so. I cannot promise that that will put to rest any spirits that abide here."

"It will make me feel better regardless," said Olivia. "Is there some other blessing that you know that would put the spirits to rest?" she asked.

"No," said Rev. Handy. "I do not delve into such things. It is beyond the scope of my education."

"I will be happy to have a blessing then," said Olivia.

The Reverend finished his coffee and they chatted about what news he had of the Potts and about new settlers in the territory. Finally, the time came to do the blessing. The reverend reached for his book, and it wasn't there. "I packed it right here," he said.

"I'm sure you did," said Olivia. "This is exactly the type of tricks they play. They will move things and hide things, and then later, they will return them."

Reverend Handy looked at Olivia as if she had spun her head around on her own body. He was horrified. He had been humoring her about the spirits, but this was more than he was prepared to deal with. He arose and walked quickly to his horse, which was still tied to the first hitching post.

Olivia hurried after him. "You're still going to bless the house, aren't you?" she called.

"Without my book?" he asked in horror. "I don't understand what is happening here," he said. "I do not have the training for this."

"Please, just come back on the porch," cried Olivia. "We'll find your book. It is here somewhere. I know it is. Give me a few minutes to look around. I know where they like to hide things."

The Reverend came back to the porch. He didn't sit, but he indicated he was willing to wait while Olivia looked for his book. He looked again in his bag, and miraculously, the book had re-appeared. His face went white, and he sat down on the porch.

"I seem to have a lot to learn, Ms. Olivia," he said in a small whisper of a voice. "You really do have spirits here. You may need more than a blessing, but the least I can do is bless this house, all those in it, and all its surroundings."

Olivia held her chest and breathed yet another sigh of relief. A man of the cloth believed her and was on her side. Things would have to improve now. Reverend Handy began to say prayers over the house and the yard. He went inside and said prayers over the whole inside of the house. They were good prayers. Olivia could feel it.

When he was finished, he took his leave. He wanted to be at the new Fort before nightfall. He could not be persuaded to stay the night. He wished them the best of luck and departed with enough sunlight to make it to the Fort with time to spare.

Olivia knew the blessing would not rid the place of the spirits. She sat down and told herself it would be alright. They meant no harm. She could see that they meant no harm. All they had ever done was to move things and appear as shadows. They had never hurt anyone. Except that they might be making her crazy.

Albert made it back, and with him came a cookstove and a bathtub. They immediately set about creating a bathhouse close enough to the house to be convenient, but far enough away to use the wastewater for the gardens. Albert was again the king of the world.

He kept on a couple of the cowboys he had hired for the drive. They built a bunkhouse for the hands, though Charlie still slept in the main house. After the bunkhouse was finished, Albert decided to add another room to the home. It would now be more of an L shape with a large wrap around porch almost as big as the house itself. It didn't take long with help from the hired hands and the men at Ft. Fitzhugh. There was a little town that was growing around Ft Fitzhugh now. It was only four miles away, so they were able to get supplies without making the long trip in to the east. It was an improvement not to have to spend two days to get supplies. It was even better not having to worry about being attacked by the Kiowa or Comanche.

There was a big feast the day they raised the roof on the new room addition. Everyone from Pottsboro, as it was now called, came in to help and to celebrate. Many of the recent arrival settlers from around Ft Fitzhugh came, too. The county was growing up. The frontier was getting tamer.

The next year, Olivia gave birth to a healthy baby girl. Albert was disappointed at first, but she won him over fast enough. The child was beautiful and rarely cried. Olivia named her Alberta. Who had her mother's eyes. Albert was pleased. Hopefully, she would not know the hardships that her parents and older brothers had known.

There was a small wagon station to the west of them now, and that meant that civilization was catching up with them. There was often merchandise at the Potts General store. Mrs. Potts would order things that she knew Olivia would like. There was even a Doctor that made the rounds to the various outposts and wagon stations.

The spirits had become part of the house now, like the floors and the walls, though the activity, generally, was in the main house leaving strangers alone. Olivia had used her white sage to no avail. She came to believe that the spirits were more like guardians and accepted them as such. She would sometimes talk to them when no one was around to hear it.

They would tell her when to plant certain things and when the Blue Northers were coming. She was happy to have their company even though she couldn't tell anyone about them.

In another year, she had a baby boy. Albert was quick to name him Oliver. It was a hard birth, and they thought they might lose Olivia the first night, but she recovered. She had to take it easy for longer than she liked, but eventually, she was back to her old self.

Albert was so proud to have a new son. Tom and Mark were better helpers than he had ever hoped for. He thought of them as his own but had secretly longed for a son. Olivia had given him everything he had asked for and more. She was the best thing that had ever happened to Albert and the thought of losing her struck him hard. He made up his mind there would be no more children for the two of them.

He never let her know that he heard her talking to the spirits. If she wanted it to be a secret, who was he to argue. They still played tricks on him from time to time, and he felt the same way Olivia did, as long as they weren't hurting anyone, he could live with them. At least she had given up trying all those rituals and potions from back east.

Oliver was crawling by Fall. Olivia had her hands full. Alberta was some help as she was able to keep the little one busy playing. Charlie had become Olivia's right hand, and she pitched in with the kids like they were her own.

Winter was coming, and Olivia was busy canning the fall harvest. She had every hand working. If you weren't peeling you better be cutting. If you weren't cutting you better be chopping wood. They had a good crop of peanuts this year, and she was boiling and canning those as well as potatoes, tomatoes, and green beans, all from the family garden. The real harvest had already been traded at market. The pecan trees had also been generous this year. There would be more than a few pecan pies this Christmas.

Albert decided well into day two of canning that it was an excellent opportunity to take Mark and Tom out Dove hunting. They hadn't been in a while, and he knew how the boys loved it. Albert thought they might need rescuing from Olivia's mad canning frenzy.

They went a little north and west to a spot near the Red River that he liked. They tied their horses and crept toward the river. Albert had Mark run into a clearing to see if there were any birds. There were, and Albert got one. Tom got the other. Mark ran towards the river to find the birds when he stopped in his tracks. Albert and Tom looked up to see what was wrong. Crossing the river were Comanche or Kiowa, it was hard to tell at this distance. Albert whistled Mark to come back. They left the birds, found their horses, and took off for home.

Comanche crossing the river was not a good sign. They fired off shots as they approached the homestead.

"Comanches!" Albert yelled as he let his horse go to the stable. Everyone abandoned what they were doing and ran for their shotguns and side-arms. Albert sent one of the boys out to Ft Fitzhugh to sound the alarm there. It would take more than two hours for help to arrive, but at least the Fort would know what was happening.

The Comanches had lost the element of surprise, and to make matters worse for them, it began to snow. The wind came out of nowhere and within fifteen minutes, it was a blizzard. The Comanche pulled back and disappeared into the snow.

Albert took a minute to check on the family and then to see to the ranch. None of the hands had been hit. There was a fire started in the barn, but it was quickly put out. The damage was minimal. He had everyone draw back to the main house. They would all be sleeping in there tonight.

They set up watch, and finally, Albert went to Olivia. She looked like she was about to faint. She looked from Albert to Tom to Mark, who lay on the floor, having taken an arrow to the leg. The boy had not said a word and put the lives of everyone there ahead of his own.

The bleeding was heavy. Albert could tell that if he took the arrow out, Mark would bleed to death in an hour. If he didn't remove it... He broke it off and left it in.

"We have to get the arrow out," wept Olivia.

"If we pull it out, he's sure to die," said Albert. "We'll tie the leg off and see if we can get the bleeding to stop. It's all we can do for now."

The snow came down hard for hours. It was what folks called a Blue Norther. He had seen the temperature drop before from Eighty to freezing in less than an hour. But it wasn't freezing yet. The snow was piling up outside. Charlie sent someone out for water. They already had a good pile of firewood on the porch for the canning. They had the fires going, and the house was plenty warm.

They settled in for the night. Olivia sat by Mark. She held his hand and tried to be soothing. He fell asleep, and Olivia let out a yelp. She thought he had died. Albert made her get up. She went into the pantry and brought out some herbs to make a poultice. It may not help, but it couldn't hurt. She also opened some chicken broth and heated it for him. She thought about the chickens.

"What about the chickens? They'll freeze," she whispered.

"They will or they won't. I'm not sending anyone else out there until we can see."

"There's a light coming from the bunkhouse," said whoever was on watch. Everyone went to look.

"Is it on fire?" someone asked.

"Don't seem to be," was the response.

"Who's missing?" said Albert.

"Jake?" said a man known as Holler.

There was no answer.

"Must be Jake," said Albert. "I'll go get him. And yes, Olivia, if I see a chicken, I'll grab it. Tend to Mark. I won't be long."

"I'll go with you to cover you," said Holler.

The two men stepped out into the wind, and it took two men to close the door. They could barely be seen in the snow. It was coming down that hard still. Olivia saw the entrance to the bunkhouse open, and two men slipped in then it closed back. Everyone in the house was watching. No one said a word. Minutes passed and they started to worry about what was taking so long. The light went dim. An hour ago, it had still been day, but might as well have been night for the blizzard. Now the snow slowed down and the daylight started to come back. They had forgotten it was still day, though it wouldn't be for long.

The door to the bunkhouse opened. Three men emerged. One was carrying another man. The newly fallen snow was still blowing and made it hard to see the details. It was almost as if they were still in a blizzard, but with a little more light.

The group in the house watched the men cross the yard to the house. It was a Comanche. Jake was carrying a Comanche. Turned out, they had both sought shelter in the bunkhouse, and neither of them was intent on killing the other so much as they were on getting warm. Jake had not even seen the Indian until he had the fire going. The Indian had been shot in the leg and was bleeding pretty bad. Not as bad as Mark, but it seemed the bullet was still in there, so he was probably in worse shape.

The men weren't sure what to do. This was the enemy. But he was injured, and it wouldn't do to just kill him, would it? Olivia told them to lay him next to Mark, and she would tend to him. He was someone's son, and she would not idly watch him bleed to death. They did as she instructed.

The Comanche was as stunned as they were. He pulled a knife from who knows where and waved it in her face as if to stab her. She slapped his hand, grabbed the blade, and threw it on the floor. The men looked on in amazement.

It grew dark. This time because the sun was going down. Olivia tended to the two wounded boys and left the food situation up to the men. They came up with beans and jerky. Someone made a plate for Olivia. While she was eating, the Indian boy died. He had been bleeding worse than they could see.

Albert decided that it would be best for one of the hands to stay here in the house and the rest to head back to the bunkhouse. They would keep an eye out on each other that way and change up watch every two hours. The men hated leaving the warmth of the home, but it was getting kind of close in the house and they looked forward to their own bunks. They moved the Comanche boy's body out to the porch.

The night passed quietly, and Albert was surprised to find the Comanche boy was gone when he stepped outside at daybreak. A rooster crowed, and Olivia breathed a sigh. If he had made it, then so had some of the hens. She went to change Mark's bandages and found that he was cold. She screamed, and Albert ran back to her. Most of the hands came running from the bunkhouse. Olivia just kept screaming. Albert tried to calm her, but she screamed until she had no voice left to scream with, then started to cry. She sat there and held him until Albert wrestled his lifeless body away from her.

She cried for all the times she should have and couldn't. She cried for all the death this land dished out. She cried for all the mothers that had lost their sons to the frontier. Then, as if a spigot had been turned, she stopped. She raised herself up and walked over to where Mark's body lay on the floor. She looked, then turned, and quietly cleared the table. Raising Mark up like he was a feather, she laid him on the table and began to wash him. She took her time. She was oh so gentle while combing his hair. She wrapped him in a sheet and stitched it up. She didn't look at anyone. She didn't speak. They let her do what she needed to do. When she had finished, she walked in a daze into the bedroom and collapsed to the floor.

Albert rushed to her, picked her up, and gently laid her in their bed. She would sleep now. He carried Mark's body out to the wagon. The snow was deep, but the sun was shining now. He would build a box for him after breakfast. He told Holler to get someone to dig the grave before the ground got too hard from the cold.

Charlie took care of the little ones and made breakfast for the family. Tom was in shock. He barely touched breakfast and had nothing to say. Your baby brother isn't supposed to die.

The house was solemn. Albert tried to find something to talk about, but all he could think of was poor Mark and poor Olivia. He wanted desperately to fix this for her, but he knew he couldn't.

Olivia slept all day and into the next. When she rose, she seemed to be in a dream. She walked to the stove and started to make breakfast, but Charlie told her that they had already had breakfast. Charlie had a stew cooking for later. Oliver was napping, and Alberta was playing in the sitting room.

"Where is Albert? I need to talk to him. I had a nightmare."

"I'll go get him, Miss Olivia," Charlie said and slipped out the front door.

Olivia looked around and started to think that maybe it hadn't been a nightmare. The reality of it came rushing in, and as Albert walked in the door, Olivia fainted. Albert carried her back to the bed. Charlie brought a wet washcloth. Albert walked to the dresser and brought out the jug of whiskey. He poured Olivia a glass and insisted that she drink it. She protested, but he would not hear "no."

He held her hand and told her how sorry he was. She asked for Tom, and Charlie brought him. Olivia held him tight. She held him until the whiskey worked. Then she drifted back to sleep.

"Is she gonna' be alright, Mr. Dixon?" asked Charlie.

"She needs time, Charlie. She's a strong woman. She wasn't ready for this. No one ever is."

"I'll be here for her and the kids, Mr. Dixon. Don't you worry about them," said Charlie.

The next time Olivia woke, it was morning. It had been three days since Mark died. The snow was almost melted, and there had been visitors from the fort. They had had to wait for the storm to pass before they could make their way out. They had come as quick as they could. They would take word back about Mark and send a preacher to say words over him. That was at the end of day one.

Now it was day three, and a rider came in to let them know the preacher could be there the next day. They had the grave ready when he arrived. Olivia was able to stand for the burial. She had no more tears to shed. She stared off to something only she could see like it wasn't even her standing there.

She went back into the house and sat in the rocker for the rest of the day. It made Charlie nervous to see her like this. She'd never known Miss Olivia to be so distant. It didn't seem like sadness. She just didn't seem to really be there.

Albert was getting concerned, too. He would hear Olivia talking to people and thought he heard her talking to Mark as if he were sitting there with her. After a week, he decided it was time to get her out of the house. He and Charlie helped her get dressed and Albert took her all the way to Potts store. They took the new buggy so as to make it a faster trip. Holler rode horseback to watch for Comanche.

"Livvy, what can I do to help you with this?" asked Albert sincerely as they rode along the now well-worn trail east.

"I don't know what you mean," she said.

"Livvy, you're not yourself. I understand you need to grieve for Mark. We all do. But you have people who are still alive, and they need you."

"I'll try to be better," she said without conviction.

"I want to help you, Livvy. I want you to be able to talk to me. I want you to be able to talk to your kids and Charlie. I want you to not have to spend your days talking to spirits."

"They're the only ones who understand," she said.

"How do you know?" said Albert. "Give me a chance to understand. Talk to me," he pleaded.

"I just feel used up, like I got nothin' left in me to give," she said.

"You shouldn't feel that way, darlin'," he said.

"I knew you wouldn't understand," she said as her head sunk to her chest.

"I want to understand," he said, realizing he had screwed that up. "Tell me why you feel that way," he said trying to recover the moment.

"The spirits tell me that it would be easier if I were with them. They say I don't need to be hurting. I could just come and join them."

"That does it!" said Albert in his sternest voice. "The ghosts have got to go! I'm going to find someone who can get rid of them. No more sage and prayin'. We're going to find someone to take care of it for good."

"But. But what about Mark? I don't want to lose him again." Olivia was finally showing some emotion.

"Well, we'll just have to make sure that he's protected," he said. "I want you here, and the kids want you here. You don't need to be thinkin' about joinin' no spirits."

Olivia leaned in to rest her head on his shoulder. Her eyes started to water, and she cried for the first time since Mark died. She thought she had cried it all out, but she had more.

By the time they got to the Potts' place, it was almost dark. They were in the shortest days of the year and it got dark way too early. Mrs. Potts was happy to see Olivia and invited them in for dinner. She also offered to let them spend the night. They agreed and were grateful for the room. Mrs. Potts had a lot of new fabric she wanted to show Olivia. Sewing would make the long cold nights go somewhat faster, she thought.

Albert and Mr. Potts sat by the fire. Albert asked if Mr. Potts knew of a Chickasaw Medicine Man.

"Well, Albert, we've got a Doctor that comes through here once a week. Why would you want a medicine man?"

"Ghosts," said Albert. "I need something to convince Olivia that the ghosts are gone. I thought maybe a medicine man could do a good ritual and get rid of 'em."

"You don't really believe there are ghosts there, do you?" said Mr. Potts.

"No, of course not. But Olivia does and with Mark being killed and all. I'd like to make her feel easier around the place."

"Can you stay through tomorrow while I see what I can find out?" asked Mr. Potts.

"Whatever it takes," said Albert feeling much better about the whole situation. Chickasaw were all about the Great Spirit. So, he figured they could help for sure.

Olivia was starting to talk like her old self here with the Potts's. She had found several pieces of fabric that she thought would look good on the kids, and she felt that Albert could use a new shirt or two. It was no trouble convincing her to stay another day.

A man of great resources, Mr. Potts found a medicine man and introduced him to Albert. The man spoke enough English to communicate and agreed to travel with Albert to his home. He had a horse and all the supplies he would need to send the spirits on to the next world.

After saying their goodbyes to the Potts', they left the next morning. It took most of daylight to get home, even using the buggy. When they arrived with a medicine man, you could hear the surprise in the voices of the cowboys. Everyone stepped back and made, room as he dismounted and walked the yard and around the house.

He started to sing in a language that none there understood. He raised his staff in one hand and a medicine bag in the other and danced and sang around the entirety of the main house. When he was finished, he sat on the porch.

"Is that it?" asked Albert. It had been a long song and an extensive dance, but the man hadn't even been inside the house.

"That for my safe," said Eye That Wanders. "Many spirits here. Some not happy. Me help. It take time."

Charlie could not believe the difference in Miss Olivia. She was talking to the babies and almost excited about the fabric she had bought. Having an Indian on the place didn't make Charlie happy, but if it helped Miss Olivia, she would be okay with it.

"Listen up!" yelled Albert. "This here is Eye That Wanders. He's Chickasaw, and we got no beef with them. He's also a Medicine Man. He's here to get rid of some nasty stuff left by those Comanche last week. Ya'll just stay out of his way, but give him anything he needs."

Eye That Wanders started to pitch a small teepee for the night. He had no desire to sleep in the cabin or the bunkhouse with these people. He made up his camp near the woods. He was close enough to know what they were doing and far enough away to keep them out of his way. When he had his camp made, he walked to the cabin. Several men had been watching him so they called out for Albert. Albert came out and welcomed the medicine man and invited him in.

Eye That Wanders shoved a suede bag in Albert's hand and said, "Give this to woman. Tell her make tea and drink before sleep. I sleep now and start in morning."

"Thank you," said Albert. "I'll give it to her right now. You have a good sleep. Don't worry. You'll be safe here." It sounded lame, but he really didn't know what to say to a medicine man.

"Me Shaman. Me always safe. You sleep. Tomorrow long day."

He walked towards the teepee, but slipped into the woods.

By morning Olivia was starting to slide back into grief. She made breakfast and hugged the kids and Albert, but she wasn't as cheerful as she had been in town. Her dreams had been troublesome as if the dead were pulling her towards them. She spoke more in whispers and seemed distracted. Maybe it was the tea.

Eyes That Wander was there at first light with several bags, stones, and other tools. He walked around each room with his staff in hand. When he had surveyed the whole house, he told them to leave.

"All must go except woman," he pointed to Olivia. "She stay. She help."

They brewed many potions during the day. Eyes That Wander said many prayers and sang many songs in various places around the house. He spent most of his time in the bedroom. Olivia was bone weary by sunset, but Eyes that Wander showed no signs of stopping.

She didn't understand anything that he was saying, but she could tell that there was a struggle going on. At one point, it looked like some unseen force was trying to rip the staff from his hands. Long after nightfall, the song slowed down and became more like an Indian lullaby. Eyes That Wander sat in the middle of the main room and chanted low and slow until abruptly he stopped, stood up and walked to the door.

"Me done. Me check again tomorrow," he turned and left.

"Is it over?" asked Albert as he poked his head through the door. "Can we come back in? Are the spirits gone?"

Olivia just looked at him. She was exhausted, but she thought she might be feeling better in spite of it. "If they're not gone, they may be on the run," she said. "He'll be back in the morning."

They came in and looked around. The house smelled funny like a gypsy tent at a carnival back east. Olivia was smiling, though she didn't realize it. Oliver and Alberta ran to give her hugs. She held them like she hadn't seen them for a week. Albert thought the room felt lighter. Maybe the medicine man was for real. Albert had only found him to make Olivia feel better. He didn't really think it would change anything at the house itself. He felt himself relax for the first time in a long time, though.

During the night, Albert woke to the sight of someone by the fireplace. He could see it from the bed. He started to get up and they disappeared. So much for Eyes That Wander having changed anything. But still, it felt different. It didn't feel as depressing. He knew the shadow man, having seen him before. It didn't scare him, though it startled him a good deal. Maybe this would be enough.

Eyes That Wander came to the door long after daybreak. He walked around the house, dancing and chanting again. The Shaman lingered longest on the porch. He came inside and danced around the rooms, waving a medicine bag and sprinkling some kind of powder here and there. When he was finished, he went to Albert and held out his hand with his palm up.

"All done," he said. "You pay now."

Albert pulled two silver dollars out of his pocket and placed them in the man's hand. Eyes That Wander put them into a pouch and walked back to the door. He turned and looked at Olivia.

"Your boy say goodbye," he said.

Then he turned and looked at Albert, "Comanche boy say Thank you."

Olivia cried for a moment. She would miss the spirits but hoped it was for the best. As they walked inside, she noticed someone in the bedroom. Glancing at Albert, it was apparent he had seen it, too. She smiled.

The End

Story 2

The Lipan Apache Tribe

In the far northern edge of central Texas near where the Red River divides the state of Texas from the state of Oklahoma, there is a house that is known to be haunted. It has so much paranormal activity that people come from all over the world to spend the night in hopes of having a paranormal experience. Some of them come as teams with cars full of investigational equipment. They are looking for concrete evidence of the paranormal. They are hoping to get a spirit on video or in a picture or on a voice recorder.

Some come as couples or families in search of a real experience and maybe some answers. Some come to try to disprove the claims. Few leave without some kind of experience.

One such "party" came on a Saturday afternoon to celebrate a thirteen-year-old's birthday. It was more people than the owners usually allowed and most of the attendees were thirteen. Some would argue that that is too young to be exploring a haunted location. However, this is what the birthday girl wanted, and Mom and Dad were eager to please.

There were supposed to be fifteen people total, but at the final count, there were five chaperones and thirty teens. With so many people, it would be hard to get any substantial evidence. It would also be difficult to know if someone had a real experience. But they didn't care and were happy to be in a real haunted house. The "hunt" was only scheduled from five to seven-thirty. There was an adult team coming in at eight, and all the birthday partyers would need to be gone by then.

At thirteen, it's not easy to sit still to participate in an investigation. The chaperones gave up and found a more secluded part of the house to try to gather ghost pictures.

The hostess realized that the kids needed some direction. She may have even feared for her house with so many children in it at one time. She asked if anyone knew what a dowsing rod was. No. No one had heard of such things. Laura, the hostess, gathered them all in the living room of the primary residence and began to explain.

"Dowsing rods used to be used to find water. Some people still use them for that purpose. The rods we have here are made of copper. The reason that dowsing rods will crossover water is because of an electromagnetic field created by water. The energy of the water can actually move the rods." She was losing them with the details. They wanted to have an experience.

"Will they point us to a ghost?" someone asked.

"No, but sometimes they will let you talk with a spirit," she replied.

Everyone became quiet. Laura had their attention.

"Should we give it a try?" she asked.

The yeses were overwhelming. Everyone wanted to talk to a real spirit.

"You can only ask yes or no questions because the rods can only respond with yes or no answers," explained Laura. "First, I want to make sure that my own protective spirit is here so I ask the rods to show me where my spirit guide is. You might call them a guardian angel. I call it a spirit guide." Laura proceeded and the rods pointed to a place by her right shoulder.

"Thank you," she said. "Now show me YES." The right rod moved until it was pointing at her chest. The left rod stayed still. "Thank you. Now show me NO." The rods crossed into an X. "Thank you," she said.

"Okay, who has a question?"

"What's your name?" yelled someone.

"Remember, yes or no questions only. You might start by asking if someone wants to talk. Then find out if it's a boy. Then find out if they are over thirteen. See how it goes?" said Laura. She was impressed with the transformation she saw, from unruly children to inquisitive teens. They were quiet and attentive for the first time since they arrived.

"Are you a boy?" someone asked.

The rods crossed for no.

"Are you over thirteen?"

There was no response.

"Are you a child?"

The rods moved to yes.

"Do you speak English?"

"Good question," said Laura.

The rods crossed for no.

"That is interesting," said Laura. "They don't speak English, but they understand the questions. Very interesting."

"Did you live in this house?"

No.

"Did you live in a house near here?"

No

"Did you live in a house?" someone said, laughing.

No.

"That's crazy. Where did you live? In a tent?"

Yes

"Are you an Indian?" someone asked.

There was no response.

"Can you show us, in our minds, where you lived?" asked Laura, thinking that with this many kids, there was bound to be a few that were still open enough to "see" what the spirit wanted to show.

"I can see it," said one girl. Then several others chimed in that they could see it, too.

"It's a girl about our age and a woman and a young child and a baby. It looks like they are some kind of Indians. They are in a ravine with a stream running through it. It's wide. Really wide. There are Teepees at the top of the canyon. But there is plenty of room they could have built the whole village on the floor of the ravine where they're standing.

The kids are playing. The ground is orange, like red clay. The stream is wide in some places and almost not even there in other areas. The woman is filling skin bags with water from the stream."

"That sounds like the Red River during a drought," said Laura. "It's only a few miles from here. Is the ravine very deep?"

"Oh yes," said one of the boys. "It's probably Forty ft deep, at least. They are leaving, going back up to the village with the water."

Laura began to see it, too. It was like they were watching a movie together or one of those rides where you are carried along seeing different scenes and movie clips as you pass.

It WAS the Red River during drought. The village or camp seemed to be on the Oklahoma side, though she wasn't sure why she knew that. There was no sign of civilization anywhere. No roads, no bridge, no sign of the white man.

The village was small. There were only a handful of tents or teepees, as they were commonly called. There were two dogs running with the children of the group. There was what appeared to be a small deer on the campfire. There was also meat laid across some bushes to the side of the camp. It appeared to be drying in the sun. Maybe this was how they made beef jerky.

"Is that where you live?" asked the child who was holding the rods.

The rods crossed for no.

"That must be why the group is so small," said a small voice from the corner. "They must be traveling or on a hunt."

"Why would they bring children on a hunt?" someone asked.

"Is that your whole tribe?"

The rods crossed for no.

"Are you on a hunt?"

No

"Are you going to join up with your tribe?"

Yes

"But why is she here? What happened to make her a ghost?" someone asked.

The scene changed, and they were back on the floor of the Red River. It was the girl and her family again. The kids were playing in the water which was towards the middle of what they had thought was a ravine. A man who seemed to be from their tribe appeared at the top of the hill. He was on horseback. He was waving at them and yelling something, but it was too far away, and they couldn't make out what he was saying.

He gestured for them to come up to the village. They didn't really want to leave yet. The mother walked out to the children to get them to get out of the water. As they were coming up, she looked upstream, and her face changed. She looked terrified like they were being attacked. Maybe another tribe was raiding them from the riverbed?

Now they could see it from the Indian girl's vantage point. There was a wall of branches and tree limbs and what appeared to be whole trees and everything else that had been loose on the riverbed. It was moving towards them with unbelievable speed. This high wall was as tall as the river bed, where they stood mesmerized for a few seconds. Then the woman shouted, "RUN!" They started to run for the side of the river. If they were fast enough, maybe they could make it out. Most of the village had now come to the edge of the top of the riverbank. They were waving their arms frantically and yelling.

The people had seen storms to the far west, but no one thought of that, causing a flood here. They had heard of such things from the elder storytellers, but no one had seen it before. One of the men tied a rope to a tree, hoping that the family would make it to the side and be able to use the line to survive.

The river was picking up more and more bushes and trees. They were not fast enough. They were overtaken by the wall which held them on its leading edge for what felt like a lifetime of terror. Finally, it swallowed them into the debris under the water that was thrusting them both down and forward. They were part of the river now.

****

Several of the children were crying, and the boy who had been so eager to use the rods had thrown them down. He didn't want to see any more.

In that instant, where so many were crying and all were in shock from what most of them had just witnessed, the door flung open and started the screaming all over again. It was the host of the adult team that would be investigating that night. Right behind her came the chaperones. They gathered the children up and herded them out to the cars.

As they drove off, the children could see the native family waving goodbye.

"Are we near the Red River?" asked one of the kids.

"Pretty close. Would you like to go see it? It's just a few minutes from here."

"NO!!!!!!!" shouted the children simultaneously. They had seen enough of the Red River for that day.

The End

Story 3

The Marshal, part 1

US Marshal Hollister Green was on a mission. He knew there was corruption in every aspect of the old town south of the state line. He knew that law enforcement was casting a blind eye on the problem. But this time... **this time...** he had them. There was proof in his pocket. The witnesses were unimpeachable. There would be no doubt. The liquor was flowing freely in Gainesville and he had the details.

He had been cautious when securing his train ticket. No one could know that he was heading to Texas. His testimony today was far too important for him to be stopped or waylaid along the way. So, he had waited until the last minute to purchase a ticket on the northbound train then get off at the first stop and buy a ticket to Texas. No one would know he was headed all the way to Gainesville.

No one would think to look for him on a train either. He left his car at home in the carriage house. No one would notice it was there. It was a good plan.

He sat back and settled in for the long ride that remained. The windows were all open, and the breeze felt good. He could feel the temperatures rising as they traveled south to Texas.

He was to be a surprise witness for the state. They had been trying to shut down this operation for years. If you wanted anything illegal brought into Texas, you moved it through Gainesville. All you needed was a lot of money and a couple of names to drop in the right places.

It was an excellent setup for the criminal element and had been since the civil war. The bad guys used much of the same routes and connections that had been used for the underground-railroad. It had worked getting the Coloreds out. It still worked. Only now it was in the opposite direction and getting the contraband in.

It wasn't just luck that had landed the Marshal in a position to have all this information. He had been working these leads for a long time, with some help from inside.

It hadn't been easy. He wasn't from Gainesville and had worked it from the supply end for a while. Then his niece married a man from Gainesville and he had a way in. This was going to break up the dirty politics and local government corruption at last.

Why did Hollister care about a town in another state? Besides being a US Marshal, he now had a relative there, and that made it a bit personal.

Emily and her husband lived in a lovely boarding house not far from the train and also close to the courthouse. They had a large suite upstairs and they only shared their bathroom with one other guest and he wasn't there much.

"Are you alright, sir?" asked a beautiful woman sitting across from him.

"Excuse me?" said the Marshal.

"You seemed to be lost in thought," she said, "but you seemed a bit distressed from the thought."

"I was thinking about my niece," he said.

"Has she caused you some problems?" asked the woman in the stylish hat and suit.

"No, no," said the Marshal. "She was a good girl. She was married to a nice young man, and they were going to have a family."

"Oh my, what happened?" she asked.

"They got involved with the wrong people," said the Marshal.

"It's going to be a long ride. Do tell," she pleaded.

"I don't know where to begin, and I don't know the whole story," he said.

"Tell me what you know," she said.

"They were living in this boarding house in town. Them and three other families plus the lady that owned the place," he started. "I had visited them there, and it was a nice enough house. They had three rooms and they even had electricity in all of them."

"As you would expect in the middle of town," she said, nudging him to continue.

"He had a job at the local hardware store as a clerk. She was involved with the church and the ladies club. They seemed happy enough."

"One day, he came home and found her strangled outside the bathroom. There was no one else in the house. It was a double tragedy because she was with child. He was devastated and hung himself days later right there in that same apartment."

"Oh my, did they catch the person who did it?" she asked.

"Not yet, but it is still being investigated. We think that her husband was in possession of some information that could be bad for local "business" if it were to get out," he said.

"That sounds most intriguing," she said. "My name is Mrs. AnnaLee Jones, by the way."

"Mrs. Jones, it's a pleasure to make your acquaintance. I am Hollister, Hollister Green."

"Well, Mr. Green, I'm delighted to have such a fascinating traveling companion. Now, tell me about this business information."

"I'm afraid I can't talk about that, Ma'am. The investigation is still ongoing, and they don't like us to talk about it."

"But surely it would be alright to tell me. I'm just a stranger on a train."

Hollister looked around the train car and was startled to find that they were the only ones in it. It struck him as a little odd that the train hadn't stopped, but the car was empty now except for the two of them.

"That's funny," said Hollister. I thought there were two gentlemen in this car with us."

"I didn't really pay any attention," said Mrs. Jones. "Do go on with your story, won't you? I believe you were about to tell me what kind of information your nephew had that would cause someone to want to kill him or his wife."

"Oh, yes. It was just some paperwork that…. well. It was just some paperwork."

"Really?" said Mrs. Jones in a shrill voice. "Someone killed your niece over some little old piece of paper? That seems harsh. Maybe she had seen something. Maybe she had seen someone doing something they shouldn't."

"Now, that's possible. She could have interrupted someone who was searching her husband's papers. It's a thought," he said as he started to think about it. His niece had been such a lovely girl. He was pretty sure that that was precisely what had happened.

Little did they know that it was Hollister who had the paperwork all along. His nephew had sent it to him immediately after finding it, knowing that it was safer with a US Marshal than in his own care.

"Ahem," coughed Mrs. Jones. "You do drift off into thought now, don't you?"

"Sorry," said Hollister. "Just thinking about your suggestion. You could be an investigator."

"Me? No. No, sir. I'm just curious and fascinated with the story. What in heaven's name do you think they were looking for that was so important?"

"It didn't matter much. They were looking in the wrong place." The words came out before he realized it. He had said too much. She may be just a stranger on a train, but it really wasn't safe yet to be talking about this to anyone not directly involved in the case. How had he let his guard down? And who was she to be asking all these questions?

"Will you excuse me for a few minutes?" she smiled as she rose and walked toward the back of the car.

As she left, two men walked in. They looked like they were from the big city back east. They drew guns and fired before he knew what hit him. They tossed his still warm body from the train as they were crossing the Red River. He technically never made it to Texas.

It is said you can see him walking the train bridge some nights. Some say you can hear him cursing himself for letting her beguile him as she had done so skillfully.

The End

Story 4

The Marshal, part 2

Approximately ninety years later:

"Did you hear that?" whispered Patty

"I didn't hear anything," whispered Brenda.

"Stop whispering!" said Mark. "You'll ruin the EVP session. I swear. You both know better."

"What did you hear, Patty?" asked Brenda.

"I heard it through the real-time recorder," said Patty. "He said "Marshal Green" clear as day."

"Roger, can you ask about it on the dowsing rods, please?" said Brenda.

"Is there someone with us named Marshal Green?" asked Roger. He was holding a set of copper dowsing rods in his hands and asking questions of the spirits that were known to be in this house.

"He said, "US"," yelled Patty.

"US? What does that mean? We're in the US," said Roger.

"US Marshal," said Patty. "He says, "US Marshall.""

"Really?" said Roger. "Are you a US Marshal?" asked Roger holding the rods steady. They moved to the yes position.

Now everyone was excited. They called in the rest of the team. Brenda brought them up to speed and started directing.

"Marybelle, can you get this on the video? "

"Mark, can you get the EMF pump set up?"

"Shelly, can you write this down as we get it?

"Roger, keep it going. Let us know if you need anything."

"Greg, we could use a second videographer."

"Everybody ready?" asked Roger. "Okay. So, you're a US Marshal. Did you die here?" The rods crossed for no.

"Did you live here?" the rods crossed for no.

"Did you die near here?" the rods crossed for no.

"Okay, this is getting us nowhere. What can I ask?" said Roger.

"Ask if someone he knew lived here," said Shelly

"Good one," said Roger. "Did someone that you know live here?"

No

"Did someone you know live near here?" Yes. Finally, they had gotten a yes!

"Did they die where they lived?" Yes.

"Was it a case you were working?" No, yes.

"Wow! Did he mean No AND yes?" said Patty.

"Did you mean to say No and Yes?" asked Roger.

The rods moved to yes. Now they were getting somewhere.

"Was it someone you knew?"

Yes

""Help me." He's saying, "help me,"" said Patty.

"You need our help? Do you want us to help you cross over?"

The rods crossed quickly for No.

"Do you want us to help you with your case?" asked Roger.

Yes and No.

"Was it a murder?" asked Roger.

The rods went straight to yes.

"Did you know the victim?"

Yes

"Were you friends?" asked Roger.

Yes and No

"Niece," yelled Patty. "He just said "niece." It must have been his niece!"

"Was it your niece?"

Yes

"Was she murdered in a house near here?"

Yes

"Were you looking for her killer when you died?"

Yes and No

"Do you want us to help find her killer?"

No

People were just asking questions now. Roger wasn't bothering to repeat the questions. The rods were just working no matter who asked the question.

"But you do want our help?"

Yes

"Is your niece here?" The rods didn't move. Dead still. Nothing.

Everyone just looked at them, waiting. He had been so communicative. Why did he just stop? Was he finished? The room got hushed while everyone tried to think of the next question.

"Do you know where your niece is?" asked Marybelle.

No

"You want us to help you find her?" said almost everyone at once.

Yes

"We're going to need a psychic medium," said Brenda. "There isn't one here tonight. Do we know anyone close?"

"There's that new girl," said Shelly. "I think she lives right here in Gainesville. What was her name? Letha? Lisa? Yes, Lisa! That was it."

"Can you call her?" asked Brenda.

"I'll sure try," said Shelly as she left the room.

"Marshal, we're trying to get someone who might be able to help find her. Can we ask some more questions while we wait?"

Yes

"Were you murdered?" asked Brenda.

Yes

"Train!" shouted Patty in a whisper.

"There's no train coming," said Mark. The house was extremely close to a train track, and everyone knew to call out "train" before one came through. The trains did a couple of things. They rattled the house and added noise to the room so that EVPs couldn't be trusted, but they also stirred up a lot of energy which the spirits would use to communicate.

"No, he **said** "train,"" said Patty.

"Was he killed by a train?"

The rods snapped to no.

"On a train," said Greg. "See if it was on a train."

"Were you killed on a train?" asked Roger.

Yes

"Was this in the Nineteen hundreds?" asked Roger

Yes

"Before nineteen-fifty?"   Yes

"Before nineteen-forty?"   Yes

"Before nineteen-thirty?"   Yes

"Before nineteen twenty?" No

"Was it in nineteen-twenty-one?"

No

"Was it in nineteen-twenty-nine?"

Yes

"Were you from Texas?"

No

"Oklahoma?"

Yes

"Who's writing this down?" asked Roger. "We have a US Marshal from Oklahoma who was killed on a train in nineteen-twenty-nine."

"Was it bound for Gainesville?"

Yes

"Folks, this is good. We can look this up. This is REALLY GOOD!!!"

"That was during prohibition," said Mark.

"Did your case have to do with prohibition?" asked Mark.

Yes

"Shelly was writing it down, and she left," said Roger, sounding a little anguished.

"I'll get it," said Mark. "US Marshal, killed on train, headed to Gainesville Tx from Oklahoma in nineteen-twenty-nine while on a case about prohibition. Got it"

"Was your niece involved in selling liquor?" someone queried.

No, snapped the rods.

"Tired. He said, "tired" just now," said Patty.

"Should we let you rest while we see if the Medium is coming?" asked Roger.

The rods moved to Yes

"Okay," said Roger. "How do we want to proceed? He wants to find his niece, and I have a lot of questions. Does anyone else have questions?"

Just then, Shelly walked back in. "Did you stop?" she asked. "Lisa is on her way over. Should I call her and tell her not to bother?"

"The Marshal is just taking a break," said Roger. "He was tired, and we want to wait for Lisa anyway."

"Aren't you afraid you won't be able to get him back?" asked Shelly in horror.

"I think he is very interested in the conversation, so I think he will be back," said Patty.

"Did we get everything on video?" asked Brenda. "Mark, will you be able to get the EVPs from Patty's recorder?"

"Everything is on video," responded Marybelle.

"I have video, too," said Greg.

"I shouldn't have any problem lifting the EVPs," said Mark. "Should we try to listen to them now?"

"No, let's not take any chances of losing anything yet," said Brenda.

Everyone sat quietly in the dark, waiting for Lisa to arrive and for the Marshal to rest up. They heard a knock at the front door, and Shelly went down to let Lisa in. You could listen to them tromping up the front stairs and chattering. Then as they should have been entering the room, no one came in, but the sounds stopped.

"Shelly?" called Brenda.

"Yes, Ma'am?" called Shelly from downstairs.

"Why did you go back downstairs?" asked Brenda.

"I came down to let Lisa in. You heard her knock, right?" answered Shelly.

"Yes, but we heard the two of you come upstairs," said Brenda.

By this time, Shelly had come silently back upstairs and gave everyone a start when she walked into the room.

"Where is Lisa?" asked everyone.

"That's what I was trying to find out," said Shelly. "Y'all heard the knock at the door, too. Didn't you?"

Everyone nodded in agreement. They had all heard it, then Shelly had gone down to let Lisa ·in.

"She wasn't there. She's not here yet," said Shelly.

"But we heard the two of you coming up the stairs. You were making all kinds of racket. Then you just got quiet."

"Well, it wasn't us. I decided to wait downstairs for Lisa."

"Maybe it was the Marshal," said Mark. Mark was the group's skeptic, so he could hardly believe the words coming from his mouth, but he had heard it like everyone else. What in the world was going on?

"Knock, Knock, Knock" This time, it was loud and came from downstairs, for sure.

"I'm not going down there by myself," said Shelly. "Not with what you just told me."

"I'll come with you," said Roger. "Let's go."

Everyone listened to them go quietly down the stairs. They heard the front door open and listened as Roger brought Lisa up to speed on the current situation as they climbed the stairs.

"Okay. Is anyone else even a little freaked out by what happened on the staircase? We all heard it, didn't we? We all heard two people coming up those stairs when, in reality, there was no one there?" asked Greg.

"Marybelle, can you back up the video and see if the camera caught the noise?" asked Brenda

"Already on it," said Marybelle.

Everyone gathered round to see and especially **hear** the playback. There were gasps from almost everyone as they listened to exactly what they had all heard. The camera had caught it. This was incredible. They had video evidence and several eyewitnesses to something extremely paranormal.

"tap, tap, tap," came a sound from the closet door.

"Start the video recorder again," yelled Brenda.

Roger raised the dowsing rods, as everyone manned their instruments. Lisa sat down to center herself.

"tap, tap, tap," came the sound again.

Greg was closest to the closet door, so he reached over and opened it. The inside of the door was a full-length mirror. A young woman and a middle-aged man were standing in it. Several people gasped and Lisa went white.

"Marshal, are you back with us?" asked Roger.

Yes

"Is that your niece in the mirror?"

Yes

"Can you talk to us through Lisa?"

No

"Dang! Can you talk to your niece?"

Yes

Everyone watched the mirror as the woman turned towards the room and seemed to be talking to someone. Lisa had gotten her color back and began to speak. "Uncle, you came too late. They wanted to know where the papers were, and I didn't know, and they didn't believe me," channeled Lisa.

"Help her," cried Patty. "He's asking us to help her."

Lisa snapped out of it and began to talk to the woman, "You don't have to stay here. Your Uncle knows what happened will take it from here. You can move on."

Lisa's neck stiffened, "My uncle only knows part. He doesn't know that my husband was killed."

Roger's dowsing rods began to spin. The girl and the man started to fade in the mirror. Lisa went limp, and Greg scooped her up and laid her gently on the bed. Meanwhile, Patty and Shelly were crying. They had never had so much activity at one time before, but it didn't feel like they were finished. There were so many loose ends. Had the

Marshal's niece crossed over? It didn't feel like it. Who was the man in the mirror?

"Roger re-gained control of the dowsing rods and began to ask questions, "Did your niece cross over just then?" No "Was that her husband with her?" No "Was it her Killer?" no answer.

Shelly was writing it all down. They were going to be doing evidence review for months on this one.

"Did you know that her husband had been killed?"

No

"suicide!" yelled Patty. "He said, "suicide." It must have appeared that her husband committed suicide after she was murdered."

Roger's rods went to Yes.

The closet door slammed shut. Everyone jumped. "What should we do?" said Greg.

"Let's see if the Marshall still wants to talk with us," said Roger. "Marshal, are you still here?"

Yes.

"Did that help you?" asked Roger.

Yes

"Do you still need to talk to your niece?"

Yes

"Do you need us to help with that?"

No

"Do you want us to help with anything else?"

Yes No

"Do you want us to come back in a few weeks?"

Yes

They came back many times, but they never reencountered the Marshal. They talk about that night to this day.

The End

Story 5

The Circus Clown

"I will not have another elephant in the back yard!" yelled David. "I'm putting my foot down on this one. One elephant is bad enough. I won't take in another."

"But the circus needs it, Papa," pleaded Kim. "And there is no room at Jeffrey's house for it. It will only be for a few days until we can find a permanent home for it."

"That's what you said about the one that's back there now!" yelled David. "I am more than happy to perform on the high wire for this circus, but I will not house the elephants. No one needs that much manure!"

"Papa, one week. Give us one week to find a place for both of them," Kim snuggled up to him and, as usual, melted his heart with her puppy dog eyes.

"One week," David relented. "Then they have to be gone," he said, knowing that he was about to be housing two elephants for the duration.

The fact that the little town had a circus was odd enough, but the fact that many of the town's people had parts to play in the circus was very rare indeed. It was not unusual to see circus animals in people's back yards. Even though the circus was housed at Leonard Park, many of the town's folk kept animals at their homes that could not be kept on the circus grounds.

The elephant's "area" was not yet complete, and David **did** want to help. This was the town's way of coping with the Great Depression, as it would later be called. The circus gave the local economy many jobs and generated a healthy income. It brought everyone together in a time when they were often looking for their next meal.

David had learned to walk the tightrope because no one else wanted to do it. He still used a net, but rarely needed it anymore. There were four trapeze artists, and they would often rehearse their acts together. David enjoyed the rehearsals as much as he did the actual performances.

Kim had known he would say yes, and he listened as they moved the giant beast into the back yard. They had walked him over from the circus grounds. He had, no doubt, wandered off during the night. Fortunately, everyone in the area knew exactly where to return exotic animals.

"Dad, we're going to go practice our trapeze act, then I'm going over to help with the new clown trainees, OK?" Kim called out to David.

"What about this new elephant?" said David. Kim was already gone. She was the youngest trapeze artist at fourteen. She had wanted to be a clown, but it turned out she was a natural on the trapeze. So, she performed on the trapeze, but helped the clowns with makeup and costuming. She knew everyone involved in the circus, and they all loved her. David smiled, just thinking about her.

They would be taking the show on the road soon. The Circus had dates set in six different cities in three states. This would be the longest run they had ever done. Everyone was excited. The circus had saved the town's economy, and many people were still in their homes because of the success of the circus. Like everyone else in town, David was quite proud of his work.

They would use the local train to move most of the animals and some of the equipment. They would play towns that were also on the train route. There were advantages to being a railway hub. Gainesville, Texas, was a perfect location as a home base for them.

"Dad?" yelled Kim. "Are you here?" Kim pulled him out of his mental meandering.

"I'm in the living room. What's up?"

"Something's wrong at the circus," Kim said. "Mr. Hollis was supposed to be there for practice, and no one can find him. Do you have any ideas? We already called his house. There was no answer."

"That's not like Tom, is it?" said David. "Do you want me to come over to spot for you until he shows up?"

"Oh, would you, Dad?" she said sweetly. "We hate to waste a practice. And I'm due at clown school in less than an hour."

"Well, then let's drive. Go get in the car. I'll get my keys," said David.

When they arrived at the circus grounds, there was a police car parked by the monkey cages. "What's going on?" Dave asked as he walked up.

"We're conducting an investigation," said Officer White. "Tom Hollis was found dead this afternoon an' it don't look like it was natural causes if you catch my meanin'."

"Where did this happen?" asked David. "Was it here on the circus grounds?"

"No," said Officer White. "He was found in a house over on Denton Street. Weren't his house. Still tryin' to figger out why he was there."

"Well, whose house is it?" asked David.

"I'll ask the questions," protested Officer White. "That's actually why I'm here. That house don't have the best reputation. It's kind of a Boarding house for single women, and you'll notice that I didn't say, ladies." He winked.

David pulled the officer aside so they could talk a little more privately. "I'll thank you not to talk about that kind of thing in front of my daughter," he said.

"Sorry," said Officer White, almost in a whisper. "I'm just tryin' to figger out where to start lookin'. One of the "ladies" said there was a clown from the circus downstairs when she took a gentleman caller up to the upstairs sitting room. She never saw Tom 'til he was laid out on the floor when she come back down. She called headquarters. She said there weren't no one else in the house. So, I guess we're lookin' fer a clown."

"Maybe we can help with that. You see, each clown has a different and unique face paint. If she can describe him, we might be able to determine who it was."

"She did describe him," Officer White leafed through his notebook. "Here it is. The witness said he was dressed in a clown outfit with orange hair and really big shoes."

"We might need a little more than that," said David. "Was he a sad clown or a happy clown? Did he have a teardrop? Did he have a hat? What shape were his eyebrows? There are lots of questions to be asked."

"She didn't remember none of that," said Officer White. "She just knew he looked like a clown."

"Maybe you could go talk to her again and ask her a few more questions about his makeup. Why would a clown have been there anyway? Our clowns don't leave the circus in costume. It's not allowed unless we're doing a show. And we're not doing a parade or a show today. Have you contacted Morton Smith, the founder?"

"Not yet. I was hoping to catch him here," said Officer White. "No one has seen him, though."

"He's probably at his house," said David. "There's a full rehearsal this weekend, and he's probably taking some time off in the mean time. I know I am."

"I'll head over there and see if he's home," said Officer White.

"I'll go talk to the people that are here and explain what's going on," said David.

Kim was crying, and everyone else was either sniffling or dumbfounded. David walked over to his daughter and gave her a hug. "Maybe we should all gather in the big tent. I'm sure Mr. Smith will be here as soon as he gets the news. We can wait for him there." They all walked to the big tent and found seats. No one was in full dress. The dress rehearsal wasn't until Saturday. Even the clowns were dressed down. "How many clowns do we have?" he whispered to Kim.

"Four regulars and three in training. Why?" she asked.

"How many of those are here?" he asked.

Kim looked around. The clowns and the trainees were all seated together. They were going to be working on makeup for the trainees this afternoon. Everyone was there. "They all are," she said.

"Interesting," mumbled David.

Morton Smith ran in yelling, "Where are the clowns? I want every clown front and center!"

The clowns all came forward. They all looked pretty upset with the situation. They had all heard about the clown being present at the house where Tom died. No one knew what to think. Most were hoping it had been a heart attack or something. No one wanted to believe that Tom had been killed. And they definitely didn't want to think that someone from the circus was involved. They were family. Maybe not blood family, but circus family ran deeper than blood.

"I'm going to want to know where each and every one of you was today. More specifically, around two-thirty PM. You all know what has happened, and we all know that it was probably a clown. We just need to find out which one."

"I would like to have that information myself," said Officer White walking in through the main entrance. "Also, do you have any pictures of your clowns in full costume and makeup?"

"Yes," said Mr. Smith. "We use them for promotional material. I'll get you copies of all of them."

"I'll be talking to each of the clowns individually. I'd like you all to stay here while I do my interviews."

"Everyone? Or just the clowns need to stay here?" asked Mr. Smith.

"Just the clowns for now," replied Officer White. "I expect I'll be talking to everyone eventually. I'd also like to know if anyone saw Tom this morning. If you saw him, just come on over and let me know." Three people raised their hands and moved in the officer's direction. Morton Smith left for his office to get pictures of each of the clowns. It made sense to let the girl see everyone in makeup. He should have thought of it and had the pictures in hand when the officer showed up.

Officer White was interviewing the clowns when Morton walked reappeared. White had already taken the names of the people who had seen Tom this morning. David walked over to Morton and asked, "Do the rest of us need to hang around, Morton? I'd like to get my daughter home. She's having a hard time dealing with this."

"Attention, everyone! Unless the officer has any objections," he said, nodding at Officer White, "I think we can all go back to what we were doing. Except for the clowns and the trapeze rehearsal. Trapeze artists meet me in the dressing room. We still have a show to get ready for. We'll get the details of Tom's visitation and funeral as soon as we have them." Officer White nodded in agreement.

David accompanied Kim to the dressing room. He didn't want her to be without him until he had a better handle on how she was feeling. Fourteen is very young to lose someone you know to murder. She seemed like such a grownup at times, but right now, she was his little girl.

"Who's going to take charge of this team with Tom gone?" asked Morton Smith. "How many changes will you need to make to the act? Someone speak up. I don't have all day."

"I've been doing a lot of the choreography. I guess I can take the lead," said Henry Burris. "If nobody else wants it," he said, looking around the room for someone to step forward. No one did. Henry would be in charge of the team and redoing the choreography. He had already been working it out in his mind while sitting in the big tent, waiting for direction. There would be a few parts of the routine that would just be dropped and replaced with something new. He could work it out by tomorrow. He was sure.

"Well, Henry, why don't you and your team go discuss strategy for a bit and then take the rest of the day to deal with the loss. I know everyone was fond of Tom, and this is quite a shock. Go regroup and be back here in the morning for a new practice," Mr. Smith was proud of his little pep talk. The group left. Most of them were still in disbelief that Tom was actually gone. Kim and David left together.

Officer White was finishing up with the last clown trainee when Mr. Smith brought him the publicity photos of the four clowns currently involved with the circus. He also brought two flyers of past performers who were no longer with the circus. The trainees had not yet established their makeup, so there were no pictures of them.

"I'm going from here back over to the house where he was found," said Officer White. "I'll be talking to the "ladies" and showing these pictures. Hopefully, she'll recognize someone out of here. All the clowns seem to have alibis, but we'll see."

Officer White returned to the house on Denton St. to find several ladies gathered on the porch. What a lucky stroke to catch them all together. He gathered the pictures and walked up to the porch. He spoke first to the woman who had actually seen the clown.

"I'd like for you to look at these photos and see if you can spot the clown that you saw this morning," he said to Miss Elisa as he handed her the papers.

Elisa studied them intently. "It wasn't any of these," she said. "He had hair a little like this one, but that's about it." She passed the papers around to the other girls.

"You talking about the clown that shows up here from time to time? We were just talking about him. Most of us have seen him, but we can't figure out who's been..." Lori paused for a few seconds as if searching for the right word, "entertaining him."

121

"You mean he doesn't come to visit anyone in particular?" asked Officer White.

"I mean as far as we can tell he doesn't come to visit anyone at all. It's kind of creepy, really. We've all seen him, and he don't look nothing like any of those pictures. But none of us has ever done any business with him."

"Well, ain't that curious," said Officer White. "Is everybody here that..." he paused, searching for the right word, "lives here?"

"Yes," they all chimed in together.

"And none of you have ever had dealings with this clown?"

"No," said Elisa. "We all just assumed he was there for one of the other girls all this time. That's what we've been sitting here talking about. What do you think it means, Officer?"

"It's a mystery, sure enough," said Officer White. "Has he ever said anything to any of you?"

They each thought about that for a bit. Then they started shaking their heads no. It was always when they were involved with a gentleman caller. The porch got very quiet. "I know he's real," said one of the girls. "I've seen him more than once."

Everyone agreed, but you could see the fear spreading across the porch like a breeze blowing across a stand of tall grass in waves. Who was this man? Were they all in danger? Did the clown have anything to do with Tom's death, or was it just a coincidence?

"I don't believe in coincidences," said Officer White. "There has to be a connection. I just have to find out what it is." He asked each of them to recall anything distinctive about the clown. By the time he was finished, he had a pretty clear idea of what the man had looked like in clown face.

"Who else was here that morning?" he asked.

"Just me and my gentleman caller," answered Elisa. "And of course, the rest of the girls found Tom when they came in."

"All you ladies were out together?" he asked.

"We had gone to the market for groceries and sundries," said Martha.

"And you are **sure** that everyone was there except Elisa?" he asked with suspicious emphasis.

"Oh yes," they all replied in unison.

"Did anyone else see Miss Elisa's gentleman caller?" asked Officer White.

No one answered. They all looked at each other. Was Elisa going to be a suspect now?

"Well, no matter. Just give me his name, and I'll check him out. I'm sure he will be able to tell me about the morning," said Officer White.

"Ummm.... I don't know his real name, Officer. I just call everyone John. It's easier, and they feel better about the anonymity."

"Well, you better find out how to get hold of him. With what I've just learned, that puts you and Tom in the house alone."

"Wait," said Martha. "Elisa was still upstairs when we came in. Was John still with you, Elisa?"

"No, he had already left. I was straightening my hair and makeup when you girls started screaming."

"Then you, Miss Elisa, are my prime suspect. Do not leave town. I will no doubt be back with a warrant for your arrest."

"Elisa couldn't have done this, Officer. Look at her, she's as fragile as a porcelain doll. I know her. There is no way she could have done this," said Martha.

"She's all I've got right now, Miss Martha. Unless you can find "John" to verify her story, she was in the house when it happened. I don't have proof that anyone else was here. She's my prime suspect."

"What about the clown?" asked Katie. "It could have been the clown."

"You mean the clown that only you ladies have seen and none of you have talked to? The mysterious ghost-clown?"

"Well, when you put it like that... It does sound a little thin," she said. "But you will look into it, won't you?"

"Yeah, of course, I will. Just don't let Miss Elisa leave."

Officer White headed back to the circus. He was hoping to catch Mr. Morton Smith still there. There was a light on in his office, so Officer White walked in that direction. "Anybody here?" he called as he approached the open door.

"Yeah, come on in," came the response from Mr. Smith.

"I have a description of the clown. It doesn't match any of the pictures you gave me. Can you read this over and tell me if it sounds familiar to you?"

"Sure," said Mr. Smith. He read the description, and his face started to drain of what little color he had.

"What is it?" asked Officer White.

Morton walked over to a file cabinet and found a picture. It was old and a bit yellowed. "Look at this," he said.

Officer White looked at the flyer. The clown seemed to match the ladies' description perfectly. "Where can I find him?" said Officer White. "If he's not a suspect, he may be a witness to something. He was definitely reported to be there."

"He's been dead for a couple of years. He was our first experienced clown. He taught everyone. He came to us from Florida."

"How did he die?" asked Officer White.

"There was an accident with the trapeze. He wasn't supposed to be up there. He had climbed up to have a discussion with Tom about a woman they were both seeing. So, the story goes. Tom jumped on the trapeze to get away from him. The clown lost his balance and fell backward, where there was no net. He broke his neck. But no one blamed Tom. It was an accident."

"That's impossible," said Officer White. "I have several witnesses who have seen this man at the house on Denton Street. He can't be dead. They've seen him as recently as this morning."

"I don't know what to tell you," said Morton. "He's dead. You want to take this picture over there to show around tomorrow?"

"I guess I will," said Officer White. "This is kind of a brick wall for me."

"Sometimes, you just have to chalk things up to Fate," said Morton.

"Thanks, I'll talk to you tomorrow," said Officer White.

As he walked out the door, he wondered if he could really be dealing with a ghost. Maybe a ghost with revenge on his mind. The thought bothered him. He wasn't one of those people who were afraid of clowns, but he wasn't sure how he felt about a clown ghost. He sure wished they hadn't outlawed alcohol. He could use a drink right about now. Instead, he went home. There was no point bothering the working girls until tomorrow. He wasn't in the mood for apprehending any floozies tonight.

After checking in at the station the next morning, Officer White headed over to the house on Denton Street. He didn't expect to find anyone up, but he thought he'd give it a try. To his surprise, Mrs. Dunn answered the door and invited him in. Mrs. Dunn was a colorful woman with curly red hair and perfectly applied makeup. She had a small cat in her arms as she answered the door. The cat didn't feel inclined to stay when she saw Officer White.

"Good Morning, Officer," she said cheerfully. "Would you like to come in?"

"Yes, please," he responded.

Mrs. Dunn showed him to a comfortable seat in the parlor. He was impressed with how elegant the room looked. The entryway was nice, but this room had velvet curtains and tassels on the lampshades and a beautiful Persian carpet.

"Mrs. Dunn, would it be too much to ask all the ladies to come in? I have a picture here that I'd like to show them."

"Certainly not," said Mrs. Dunn. "You wait right here. I'll see that everyone gets decent before they come down."

Officer White felt a little uneasy waiting. He had never been in a house of ill repute, and this was not what he had expected. The parlor door opened, but no one entered. It was not the door Mrs. Dunn had left through. This was a double French Door with velvet and lace covering the windows. Officer White stood slowly.

"Hello," he called. "Who's there?"

There was no answer, but the door opened wider still. Officer White moved cautiously toward the door. Before he reached it, it slammed shut. Officer White jumped. But then he continued to approach the door. He meant to find out who was there. He opened the door quietly.

"Hello?" he called again.

There was no answer. There was no one in the room beyond, either. It was a dining room. He turned to go back into the parlor. There, by the other parlor door, stood the clown. He stopped. He rubbed his eyes. The clown didn't move. Suddenly the door opened, and the clown disappeared. Mrs. Dunn slid gracefully through the door.

"They will all be down in a moment," she paused to find Mr. White no longer seated.

"Why there you are," she said as she turned to look at him. "Officer, are you feeling quite well? You seem a bit pale."

"I... I... I'm fine," he stuttered. "I just had a most remarkable experience."

"What happened?"

"Well, I don't rightly know. This door opened, but there was no one there. Then I thought I saw a clown. He was only there until you opened the door and then he was gone. I must not have gotten enough sleep last night. I must have been seeing things."

"Officer White, I do apologize. That door will open from time to time. We attribute it to a draft. And the clown is seen here frequently, though we've only just yesterday discovered that no one of us has ever talked to him."

"Is this the one you've all seen?" he produced the picture that Morton had given him the night before.

"Well, that's certainly the one I've seen," she said. "We can ask the others when they get down. I'm sure they'll be here momentarily."

As if on cue, one of the ladies walked in. Officer White showed her the picture, and she confirmed that this was who she had seen. It was the same story with each girl that entered. This man that had been dead for two years was the one that everyone here had been seeing. In fact, it was the man that he, himself, had seen with his own eyes, only minutes before.

He didn't tell them that the man they had all thought they had seen was dead. He didn't want to frighten anyone unduly. There had to be an explanation. But he couldn't think of one. He decided to swing back by the circus. Maybe Mr. Smith could shed a little light on this.

Morton Smith was in his office. There seemed to be some dispute about name placement on a banner. Mr. Smith asked everyone to leave when Officer White walked in. The office emptied immediately.

"What did you find out?" asked Mr. Smith.

"This picture you gave me? It's him. He's the one they've seen over there. Are you sure he died?"

"Oh, yes. Went to the funeral myself. The whole circus family was there. All the clowns dressed in clown face for it. Quite a tribute, it was."

"Well, then... why are they seeing him in that house, I wonder? I keep looking for a logical explanation, and I just can't find one."

"Maybe there isn't one," said Mr. Smith.

"What do you mean, no explanation? There has to be!" said Officer White.

"Bear with me. What if that clown really is a ghost? And what if that fall two years ago wasn't an accident? What if old Tom gave a little push? What if that clown has been waiting all this time to get even?"

"That's impossible!" said Officer White. "There's no such thing as ghosts, and even if there was, they couldn't break a man's neck."

"You mean that's how Tom died? His neck was broke?"

"That's what the Coroner says."

Linda Anthony Hill

"That ain't no coincidence. That was the ghost," yelled Morton Smith.

Officer White kept studying his notebook. Nothing made sense. And he couldn't forget that he had seen it for himself. He left Mr. Smith, knowing that there would be no plausible explanation for this. He would have to leave his report open without any answers.

He could only imagine how the ghost might have lured Tom up the stairs and then scared him into jumping over the rail and falling to his own death, just like the ghost had done years before.

Officer White went back to the station and wrote up his report. He left out all mention of the clown and just wrote that there were no clues to make him think that Tom hadn't accidentally fallen from the stairs above the entry, breaking his neck when he hit the floor below.

So, Tom's death was officially listed as an accident, but Officer White was never really sure, and he stayed away from the house on Denton Street for the rest of his career.

The End

Story 6

Sleep, Elizabeth

The shadows played tricks on her. They did it all the time. Ever since her father died six months ago, she had seen him in the shadows. Whenever she needed him, he would come down the hall or come round the corner and she would catch a glimpse out of the corner of her eye. But when she looked full on, he was gone.

Her husband didn't believe her. He thought she might be going mad. But he didn't fight her when she said she wanted a divorce and he agreed that the children should stay with her.

Their daughter, Elizabeth, was so sweet and had only been in school for a couple of years. She loved having Daddy stop by in the mornings and give her a lift to school. It was only a few blocks,

133

but it meant getting to see him every day and she loved that.

Their son, Richard, was a little older and more independent, but he let his dad take him to school anyway. He thought it would help his parents see that they needed to get back together. He would talk to his dad while they drove and let him know how much his mom needed him. Richard's dad would always listen. He didn't want to hurt Richard's feelings. But he knew there would be no reconciliation between Amanda and himself.

She had too many emotional problems since her dad died. He only let the kids stay with her because he knew he could keep a close eye on them. But there was no way that he could live with her anymore. She spent a lot of time crying. She didn't want him to touch her. He had tried to comfort her, but she pulled away in horror convinced that her father was watching.

"How is your mom doing?" he asked his son.

"She's been kind of quiet, Dad," Richard answered. "I think she'd be a lot better if you were there. She sits at the kitchen table and just stares off at nothing a lot."

"Maybe she's getting better," Mr. Barnes said, not really meaning it, but wanting to give Richard as much hope as he could honestly give him. "She's not crying all the time anymore, is she?"

"No, Dad. She seems pretty calm. It's like she knows everything is going to be okay." He said. "You should talk to her. You'll see. She's getting better."

"I'll take your word for it, Son," said Mr. Barnes. "Here we are. You have a good day at school and I'll see you tomorrow."

"Bye, Dad. Do you want to come over for dinner?"

"Thanks, Son, but I already have plans." Mr. Barnes hadn't told the kids yet that he was seeing someone else. There would be time for that when he knew it was actually serious. For now, he wanted to keep his kids safe from getting to know women only to lose them when Dad stopped seeing them. Perhaps he was too protective, but it was his decision and he had made it.

He drove on to work.

Amanda Barnes was sitting at the kitchen table writing a letter. She had been working on it

135

for some time. She couldn't get the wording just right. She was writing to her mother to let her know what she was planning and explaining why it made sense. She struggled with the letter all morning.

Elizabeth got out of school before Richard. They had a friend that lived across the street from the school and Elizabeth would wait for Richard there. Then the two of them would walk home. She was sitting on the porch waiting for her friend and reading a homework assignment. It was a pretty day and the porch was a comfortable place to do homework. Sometimes she and Sheri would sit on the porch to do homework before they would go inside to watch TV.

Sheri was in third grade so she was much closer to Elizabeth in age than to Richard who was in sixth grade. Sometimes she would help Elizabeth with her homework and sometimes Richard would help Sheri with **her** homework. It was a good arrangement.

Today she didn't need any help, though. She might even finish up before Sheri got there. She still needed to write about the story she had just read and answer a few questions.

She was finishing up when Sheri arrived. Elizabeth would probably just read the next chapter in her book while she waited for Sheri to finish her homework.

"Hi, Liz," said Sheri. "Have you been waiting long?"

"Long enough to get most of my homework done," said Elizabeth. "But I didn't have that much to do. And I still have to read a chapter from this book." She held up the book to show Sheri what she was reading.

"I don't have much either," said Sheri. "I can do it later if you want to go in and watch some TV first."

"That would be great!" said Elizabeth excitedly. "Is Tomorrow People on yet on Nickelodeon?"

"Let's go see," said Sheri.

It was on and they were able to watch an entire episode before Richard showed up. Sheri let Richard in and asked him if he could help her with some Math homework.

"Sure," said Richard. "We have plenty of time before we need to be home. "Elizabeth, do you have something you can work on while I help Sheri?"

137

"Yes," said Elizabeth. "I have to read a chapter in this book."

"Perfect," said Richard.

Time flew by and it was time for Richard and Elizabeth to walk on home. Their mother was still sitting at the kitchen table when they arrived. There was no dinner cooking.

"Mommy," said Elizabeth. "What's for dinner?"

"I thought we would go out for dinner," answered Amanda Barnes. "Where would you like to go?"

"McDonald's!" they yelled together. "McDonald's, McDonald's!"

"McDonald's it is," she said. "Go put your things away and then, we'll go."

They both ran to their bedrooms to put their things away so they could go before she changed her mind. McDonald's was a special treat and they loved playing in the playground after they had eaten. It was a pleasant evening for it, but they wouldn't have cared if it was one-hundred-ten. They loved playing outside in the oversized outdoor playground. They had both found friends to play with and could have stayed all night.

"Time to go," yelled their mom.

"Just a few more minutes," they begged, knowing it was useless. When mom said time to go, she meant it.

But today she surprised them. "Okay," she said. "We'll stay a little longer."

They stayed at least fifteen more minutes. Mom must finally be in a good mood again. She didn't have good days very often anymore and it made them both feel hopeful that she was having a good day today.

After they arrived home, they expected Mom to tell them to get ready for bed. Instead she told them they could stay up and watch TV as late as they wanted. "Don't we have school tomorrow?" asked Elizabeth.

"Yes, but you never go right to sleep so, tonight you get to stay up late and we'll see how long you stay up," said Mrs. Barnes.

The kids turned on the TV and fought over what to watch, but settled on a new show. After a while their Mom asked them if they were ready for baths. They agreed that they were. Elisabeth took hers first and came back in to watch some more TV. It was Richard's turn and he sped through it so

139

he could get back to his show. It was eleven o'clock when their mom finally gave them their evening meds and sent them to bed.

She sat at the kitchen table the rest of the night.

When Mr. Barnes arrived early next morning, Amanda told him that they had had a late night and the kids were taking a sick day today.

"Can I see them?" he asked.

They're both sleeping right now," she said. "I'd hate to wake them."

"I'll stop by after work to see if you need anything," he said.

"We won't," she answered.

He left for work. Amanda watched as he drove off. Then she went in and put a bullet in little Elisabeth's head. She would never have to experience the pain that Amanda had been through these last few months. She would never have to experience any pain ever again. The sound roused Richard who came in to Amanda's room to see what was going on.

"Lie down here and go back to sleep," she told him. The sleeping pills she had given them last night had worked beautifully, just like her father had said they would.

Richard lay down on his mom's bed and fell back into a deep sleep. Amanda put the letter to her mother in the mail box. She straightened up the house and put away the dishes. She sat at the kitchen table again and talked with her father for an hour. She told him how hard this was and he told her how easy it would be once she had finished. She told him it didn't feel right and he told her it wouldn't matter. She needed to go and help Richard now, before the drugs wore off.

Amanda walked into her bedroom and shot Richard in the head. She breathed a long sigh of relief. Her children were now safe. They would never know the heartbreak of loving and losing love. They would never know the pain of losing their parents.

Amanda sat back down at the kitchen table. She looked at the pawn ticket for her wedding rings. They had fetched just enough to pay for the gun and the bullets. Her children were safe now. Her children were safe now.

She picked up the gun one last time and went to her bedroom. She lay down next to her son and blew her own brains out.

* * * * * * * * * * * *

Elizabeth found herself at school. How did she get here? Where were her books? Where were her friends? It was scary being in here all alone. She wanted to go home. As if by magic, she was home. But again no one was there. It didn't feel good being at home either. Maybe her friend, Sheri was home. The magic wish worked again and she was on Sheri's front porch. There was no one there, but it felt okay.

After some time, Richard showed up.

"How did I get here?" he asked.

"It seems like magic," said Elizabeth. "Just think of where you want to be and you're there."

Richard closed his eyes and he was gone.

That was rude, thought Elizabeth. But she felt better having seen her brother. She wished she were inside hanging out with Sheri. She felt lonely and sad and a little scared again. Boom! She was inside on the couch watching TV. It wasn't the channel she wanted. She wanted channel five. The TV complied. She didn't see anyone else in the room, but she felt like there was someone there. She wished she could see them.

Magically, an old man appeared.

"Who are you?" He yelled. "Get out of my house!"

"I'm Elizabeth," she tried to tell him, but she was back on the porch. Then Richard showed up again.

"It works, but it's weird," Richard said to her.

"I'm scared," cried Elizabeth. "There's a mean old man in there that says this is his house, but it's Sheri's house, isn't it?"

"I don't know about scared," he said. "But it IS a puzzle."

"That mean old man inside shouldn't yell at people like that," Elizabeth told him. "It's not even his house."

"I'm going back to our house. I'm going to try to figure this out," said Richard.

And he was gone. Elizabeth still didn't like the feeling at home, so she decided to stay at Sheri's house. Then the old man walked out and started yelling at her. She went upstairs, but he followed her. She hid in the hall closet and tried to be as quiet as the tennis shoes she was sitting next to. She didn't want the old man to find her.

She heard the door lock from the outside. She tried the door, but it wouldn't open. The old man had locked her in. She was terrified and it was so dark in here. She abruptly fell asleep. When she woke-up she was still in the closet and could hear footsteps outside the door. She kept still, hoping she wouldn't be discovered.

The door opened. There was no one there. It had just opened on its own. She walked downstairs. She had forgotten that she could wish herself anywhere. She had forgotten a lot. She went into the room with the TV. The old man wasn't there so she turned on the TV and looked for her favorite show. She couldn't find anything she recognized so she watched something else for a while and then fell asleep again.

When she woke up it was because the old man was yelling at her again. He dragged her to the upstairs closet and locked her in again. She was now petrified. This was such a nice place until the old man showed up. She wished he would stay away.

She heard someone out in the hall. They were asking if anyone was there with them. "I'm here", she answered.

"What is your name?" they asked.

"Elizabeth," she responded.

"Do you want to hurt us?" they asked.

"Why would I want to hurt you? I'm locked in the closet."

"How old are you?" they asked.

"I'm seven," she answered. "Can you let me out?"

The door opened, but like before there was no one there. Who had she been talking to?

"Who locked you in the closet?" came a voice from thin air.

"There's a mean old man here who locks me in the closet. Why can't I see you?"

"You can't see us?" came the response.

Elizabeth jumped back in the closet, closed the door and fell promptly to sleep.

"Elizabeth?" someone said in a soft voice. "Are you here today?" It was Angie. She was a Spirit Rescuer, but Elizabeth didn't know that. She felt like she should trust the woman, though. She opened the door and saw a blonde woman sitting on the floor. She was wearing blue jeans and a shirt with a feather on it. She could see this one. It wasn't just a voice in the dark.

"Hello," said Elizabeth in a small quiet voice. "Have you seen my brother?"

"I'm here to help you," said Angie. "Do you know why you're here?"

"I'm hiding from the old man. He's mean to me."

"Would you like to be able to leave?" asked Angie.

"I like it here except for the old man," said Elizabeth.

"Is the old man always here?" asked Angie.

"No," said Elizabeth. "Sometimes my brother is here. Sometimes it's just me. Sometimes there are voices, but no people."

"You can go other places," said Angie. "You can go to the light and be free of all this or you can go to different places. But, let me tell you what you can't do."

"What?" whispered Elizabeth.

"You can't be locked in a closet or anywhere else. You are a spirit and free to come and go as you please. Would you like to try it?"

"Now?"

"Yes," said Angie. "I will lock you in the closet and you will use your thoughts to wish yourself out."

Elizabeth hesitated, "how do I know I can trust you not to lock me in the closet again?"

"I'm a good person and won't hurt you," said Angie

Elizabeth thought long and hard before she finally went into the closet.

"Now just wish yourself out here with me," said Angie and poof! Elizabeth was out in the hall.

"I remember!" she yelled. "That's how it used to be. I could wish myself places."

"That's how it is again," said Angie. "Where will you go?"

"I think I will look for my brother Richard," said Elizabeth.

"Do you think we will see you here again?" asked Angie. For the first time Elizabeth could see a lot of grown- ups sitting in the room. "Everyone here would like to be able to talk with you and play with you."

"Then I will come back. Will someone read me a story?" she asked.

"Yes, Yes, we will," said one of the grown- ups. "What story would you like to hear?"

"I kind of like Nancy Drew," said Elizabeth.

"Then we will find a Nancy Drew book to read to you," said a nice lady.

Elizabeth wished she knew where Richard was and was immediately transported to the old school. It looked old and dirty now. Richard was there sitting on the stairs.

"There's no one here," he said. "It makes me sad sometimes. I keep falling asleep and waking up upstairs in the science lab or on the front porch of Sheri's house."

"Do you still go home?" asked Elizabeth.

"No, it's very uncomfortable there. It gives me a headache."

"I found some people," said Elizabeth. "They are invisible sometimes and other times you can see them. They said they would read me a story when I come back. But I came back and they weren't even there."

"They shouldn't have lied to you," said Richard. "Maybe they will come back another day."

"I hope so," said Elizabeth.

The End

Story 7

Clowning Around

In nineteen-thirty-three there were celebrations in the streets as alcohol became legal again. The Great Depression was four years old, so the celebrating was not as festive as some would have hoped, but there was a large portion of the population that found great hope in the repeal of prohibition. Alas, the depression lasted six more years.

Those who had been earning money from illegal sales of alcohol were squeezed out. The local SpeakEasies became nothing more than neighborhood bars. Homes that had been used as SpeakEasies reverted to boarding houses for ladies of the evening and anyone else who cared to live in that environment.

Such a home was located in the downtown area of a small town near the Texas Oklahoma border. Many of the employees moved on as the environment became more boarding house than night club. For a time, it was a well-known house of ill repute. When a man was found dead in the entryway under suspicious circumstances, many of the girls became frightened of being in the place and sought work elsewhere.

Men who were down on their luck could get a room by the week in exchange for carpentry work as the home was converted into something more rentable. The downstairs was divided into two suites. Each had its own bathroom, kitchen, living room and two bedrooms with front and rear entrances. The upstairs remained available as rooms for boarding until the remodeling was complete. One of those rooms was like a bunkhouse with several beds.

Maxwell Brenner came to inquire about a room on a Friday afternoon. He was an affable man of medium build. He wore a hat that looked more like a cowboy hat than a fedora, yet he didn't act like a typical cowhand. He looked like a man who was surviving the depression one day at a time.

"I understand that a man can get room and board in exchange for work here," he said to the woman who came to the door.

"You understand correctly," said Molly Thacker with a twinkle in her eye. Maxwell was a handsome man in his thirties's, and few women could resist a little flirtation in his direction. "Allow me to get my husband. He handles the remodeling." Molly closed the door and was soon replaced by her husband, James. James was a mountain of a man. He was the kind of man who had to duck through many a doorway.

"What can you do?" James came straight to the point.

"I can drive a nail. I am also good at finish carpentry. I can carve fine details into the wood." Maxwell withdrew a knife from his belt and offered it to James. "I carved and finished this handle. I have a knack for wood."

"Anything else?" asked James. "We might need some help with plumbing."

"I can be a helper with anything," offered Maxwell without hesitation. "I've worked on lots of projects and always available to help with whatever needs doing. Plumbing is still a bit tricky but, I've been a helper on a few plumbing jobs. I can help with electrical, too. With finish carpentry, I don't need any supervision."

"Where's your bedroll?" asked James.

"I left it on the porch."

"Grab it, and I'll show you your room. Be downstairs for breakfast at seven. Be ready to start work right after that. You already missed dinner, but I'll see if Mrs. Thacker has anything leftover for you. Come back down after you get settled."

"Thank you, Mr. Thacker," said Maxwell.

"First few days are a trial," said James. "Mess up, and you'll owe me for room and board. Keep it in mind."

Maxwell opened his bedroll and set out his shaving tools and extra shirt and pants. The bed in this room had sheets and a quilt, so he rolled his bedroll back up and put it in the corner. There was a lamp in the room and curtains on the windows. This would be the nicest place he'd slept in a while.

He walked downstairs to see about that food Mr. Thacker had mentioned. Molly answered the door and ushered him into the kitchen. She had put together a sandwich out of the leftovers and had placed a glass of milk next to it at the kitchen table.

"You'll be coming down the back stairs from now on," she said. "Hired hands come to meals through the back door. You just sit down here and fill that fine stomach with a good sandwich," she coo'ed.

"Molly, leave the boy alone. Come in here and give me a foot rub. I've had a rough day," called James from the living room.

"Oh, James, I didn't mean anything by it. Just habit from the old days, I guess. He is kind of cute, though," she giggled.

"Watch yourself," said James sternly. "I'll have to remind you who you belong to when I get you in the bedroom."

Molly giggled again. She looked forward to it. He was so big and so stern that sometimes people took things the wrong way. He was just a gentle giant with Molly. He tried to act like a bear sometimes, but she saw through it. She loved him, but he was right; she did like to flirt with the young men.

Maxwell heard the exchange from the kitchen and wondered what the "old days" were exactly. He just wasn't curious enough to cross Mr. Thacker. The man was built like a brick house. No man in his right mind would want to get on that man's bad side.

"Ma'am, that was mighty good, and I do appreciate the hospitality," he said as he walked to the door. "I'll just be heading on up to my room now."

"Sweetie, let's not be so formal," said Molly. "You just call me Miss Molly. Everyone does."

Maxwell looked at James. James nodded, and Maxwell responded, "Thank you, Miss Molly. I'll see you good folks in the morning."

Maxwell wondered as he walked away why they had an open room in the house. The food was as good as he'd ever had and there was plenty of it. They had electricity and plumbing. The rooms were first rate. They should be turning workers away. *Curious*, he thought.

The bed was more comfortable than he expected and he slept through the night. The sounds of people stirring woke him up and he looked for a clock, and found none. He jumped up and dressed in a hurry just to be safe. He didn't want to be late on his first day. He opened the door to see three men in the hall. All were in various stages of being dressed.

"What time is it?" he called.

"Almost seven, buddy. You better hurry," said the one closest to him. "You're hired hand, right?"

Maxwell nodded. He ran a comb through his hair and decided to wait to shave. He went on down to the kitchen.

"I haven't rung the bell yet, sweetie," said Miss Molly. "Go on back upstairs and get your cleaning up done. I'll be ringing the bell when everything is ready."

Maxwell left and walked back upstairs. There were two using the sink to shave. He decided there might be room for one more. He fetched his shaving kit and joined in. He was just finishing up when the bell rang. No one got in a hurry. However, everyone began moving downstairs. He followed them in.

"Sit down, boys. Mr. Thacker will be right here," Miss Molly announced. "Go ahead and get you some milk. Here he is. Max, you sit over here." She pointed to a stool at the end of the table.

James sat down and added a biscuit to the plate Molly had already loaded up for him. Everyone else took that as a cue to start serving themselves. They passed around the plate of scrambled eggs, then the bacon, then the hash browns, then the biscuits and finally the gravy. It was a fine breakfast.

There was no conversation as everyone concentrated on eating. James finished and looked around to see that most everyone was finishing up.

"Let's get to work, boys," he said as he rose and started for the back door.

There were a few quick gulps of food and milk, and off they went following the big man out the back door. Maxwell just tagged along, ready for whatever the day's project was.

James looked around the tiny yard and announced that it was time to run plumbing to the kitchen of the second downstairs suite. They would tap into the bathroom from under the house and run straight up the side of the house to the front window. "That's where the sink is going," he said.

The boys all nodded but looked a bit nervous. Plumbing pipes were heavy, which made them difficult to connect. James saw the worry in everyone's eyes and said, "It'll be okay, boys. Relax. I got Ted coming over to do the joiners. We're just here for the heavy lifting."

That seemed to help. Everyone knew just enough about plumbing to know they didn't know enough.

"When is he supposed to show up?" someone asked.

"Soon as I go get him," said James. "In the meantime, you boys start taking off the skirting on this side of the house. No need working in the dark. Billy, you're in charge until I get back."

James took off to get Ted and pick up supplies for the project. He was excited about getting the suite ready to rent. He had bought the house so cheap that he had money for the fixup, but he was ready for some real money to start flowing in. This was going to be a nice apartment. He should be able to rent it for enough to finish out the upstairs next.

Ted loaded his plumbing tools into the truck, and they took off for the hardware store. Ted had already drawn a plan of what needed to be done and made a list of what they would need. There were metal pipes and elbows and connectors and t's. There were also some welding supplies, but that would come later.

It was almost ten by the time they made it to the house. The crew had the skirting off, and the crawl space was pretty good. There was easily three ft under most of the house. It was a little tighter than that where the kitchen sink would be, naturally.

"Let's get the pipes laid out first," said Ted. He pulled out his drawing for everyone to look at. "The longest one will go over here from the kitchen back to the bathroom. We can get that one lined up first."

Everyone got to work. It didn't take long to get the pipes laid out and ready. Ted crawled under the house to survey the layout before he started joining pipes. There were a couple of pieces out of place, but he chalked that up to "too many

159

cooks in the kitchen." The next step only needed two helpers under the house and one to do the cutting. The fact that he had enough helpers turned a three-day job into a one-day job. By the end of the day, all the drain pipes were in place. They would get the cold water run the next day.

"That's it for today," said Ted. "Can't tell you how much help your crew was. I might have to steal 'em from you from time to time." He was joking, but only half so.

The boys all smiled, and James made a frown jokingly. It was all light-hearted fun.

"Billy, get the boys to get the mess cleaned up while I take Ted home. Then you can all call it a day."

"New guy, look at the staircase and think about what you might do to fancy it up a bit."

James left with Ted in tow.

"They'll be stopping at the pub, I'm thinking," said one of the boys. "Guess there's no hurry getting this all cleaned up." He laughed as he said it.

Maxwell went inside to look at the stair rail. There was a chunk missing towards the top. It wasn't a big chunk, just big enough to notice. He thought he could carve a pattern into the whole banister and work that into the design.

The spindles were just a square cut. He'd need to take them all out to carve some curves and fancy flairs to them, but it was something he would enjoy. The landing Newel was nice, but he would like to carve something into it. Maybe a lion or something like that. There was a lot of room for improvement. Enough to keep him in room and board for a long stretch. He started to feel better about his situation.

Miss Molly came out of her apartment suite to see who was loitering in the entryway.

"What are you up to, sweetie?" she asked.

"Mr. Thacker asked me to look at the stairs to see what I could do to fancy them up a bit."

"Oh, that would be nice. They're very plain, aren't they?"

"They're sturdy and well built, Ma'am. They're just a little plain."

"What are you thinking?" Miss Molly asked.

"I'm thinking I'll have to take the banister off and take out all the spindles so I can turn them on a lathe to put some design in them. Might even carve some birds or animals into each of them." He was thinking out loud now. He was only barely aware that Miss Molly was there.

"That sounds wonderful," she said. "It will be nice to have a striking stairway in the entry. You need some paper to make some drawings, sweetie?" she asked.

"I suppose it would be a good idea to give you and Mr. Thacker an idea of what I'm thinking of doing. Do you have some drawing paper?"

"Of course. I'll go get you some," she said, hurrying off into the suite. She re-emerged with a notepad and a pencil. It was a good size for carrying in his shirt pocket. "Here you go. You keep this. You'll probably end up using the whole thing before you're done."

"Yes, Ma'am, I might," he mumbled as his mind started working on the staircase. He went outside to get a measuring tape. The boys had one. Back inside, he went to marking designs on the spindles themselves. He was making notes in the book and taking measurements. He reached for the measure at one point and discovered it was at the top of the staircase. *When was I up there?* he thought. *I guess I'm getting old. I sure don't remember it.*

James came home to find most of the crew out back, sipping on some homemade beer Mrs. Thacker had given them. Not everyone stopped drinking during prohibition, and Molly Thacker had learned to brew beer as a hobby that grew into a sideline during the long thirst.

James noticed that the new boy wasn't with them and asked about him.

"Oh, he's inside working on the stairs," said Miss Molly. "Well, measuring and drawing anyway. He seems pretty excited to get to work on them."

"And I suppose you were in there helping him, were you?" asked James in a voice that was not too pleased.

"No, I just brought him a notepad to sketch his design and what have you," said Miss Molly, not taking note of his tone at all. "He barely knew I was there. That's how intent he was with his project."

The crew started looking at each other, wondering if they should leave the boss to work this out with Miss Molly.

Just then, Maxwell walked out the back door. "Sweetie, do you want a beer? I'll go get you one, and you can join the boys." She hurried off to get two beers, one for James and one for Maxwell.

James just stood there. It was hard to be mad at his wife. She just didn't think like most folks. In fact, he thought that most times, she didn't think much at all.

"I hear you got some drawings to show me," he said to Maxwell.

"It's not much," said Maxwell. "I did some drawing on the stairs, too. This is sort of what I'm thinking." He pulled out the writing pad and showed the boss some pages of sketches of the birds and an eagle and one drawing of one spindle. "I'm thinking that each spindle can be similar, but a little different, like a different bird on each one and they'll look like they're flying or landing,"

"That looks like a lot of work," said James. "I wasn't planning on you being here for life." He laughed when he said it and everyone laughed with him.

Molly walked out with the beers. James and Maxwell found a seat and joined the others in conversation. Molly went back to the house to get dinner ready. She hoped that Maxwell would be around for a good long while. He was cute, and she liked him.

Dinner was spaghetti and meat sauce with meatloaf and biscuits. There was plenty, and after James was served by Molly, everyone started passing the food around the table. As always, Molly was the last to serve herself and sit down to eat. Maxwell watched her eat and wondered why such a beautiful and charming woman was so happy to keep house for all these men. He wondered if James knew how lucky he was.

James noticed Maxwell eyeing his wife and interrupted it by asking Maxwell what he would need to start the project.

James didn't care what was needed. He just wanted to redirect Maxwell's thoughts. He had dealt with many men who wanted his wife. This one was a bit young, but that never stopped a man from wanting something that wasn't his to want. The ploy worked, and Maxwell started laying out what was needed.

"First off, Mr. Thacker, do you have a lathe? That would be the only way to make those spindles look perfect. It wouldn't need to be a fancy new electric one. I can use a foot pumped one just as easy. And I'll need something to sharpen my carving tools with. And…"

"Slow down, son," said James. "I don't have a lathe, but I can get one. Are you planning to completely dismantle the staircase?"

"Yes, sir, that's the only way I know to do the spindles right. They're just two-x-two's with no decoration at all right now."

"You know a man died falling from the top of that staircase. And that was **with** a railing. I don't want no one getting hurt," said James with not a hint of a smile.

"I think we can all be careful while I'm working on it, and I can put up a temporary railing while I'm working on the spindles. I'll do them first and then the rest of the carvings I can do with them in place," Maxwell was almost pleading with Mr. Thacker to let him do this project. For some reason, it had become important to him.

"A temporary one, you say? I guess that will work." He turned his attention to Molly. "Mrs. Thacker, that was a fine meal. Let's leave the dishes to the boys here, and you and me can go out and sit on the front porch. There ought to be a good sunset tonight."

"Thank you, Mr. Thacker. That sounds lovely," she responded shyly. "Would you like a beer or a glass of wine?"

"Do you have any of your fine lemonade?" he asked.

"I do, indeed. I will pour you a glass and be right out."

Maxwell could see that Mr. Thacker actually **did** appreciate what he had. Still, he found himself thinking of her often. She was a treasure, and everyone in the house seemed to know it.

The crew made quick work of the dishes and went out to the back porch to pass the time before bed. Billy brought out a deck of cards, and everyone was ready to see how the new guy handled himself in a game of poker. He did well, but not so well as to create any enemies.

On the front porch, James and Molly sipped their lemonade and watched a particularly colorful sunset together. Their rocking chairs kept time together, and James imagined the second suite being finished and rented. It brought a smile to his face. Molly was thinking of young Maxwell, and that brought a smile to her face.

Suddenly they heard a crash from the entry. They ran in and found no one there, but in the middle of the floor was a tape measure case. "Must have fallen from the vibration of the train," said James.

"What train?" asked Molly.

She jumped at the sound of a train horn. How strange, she had not heard it coming. She must have been too deep in thought.

James laughed and said, "That one." But, in truth, he had not heard the train either. He just guessed that that could have caused the measure to fall. He wasn't really sure. The staircase had strange occurrences from time to time. He sometimes wondered if it had anything to do with that man dying there. They said it was an accident, but unofficially there was a rumor that he was killed.

This house had seen a lot of activity. It was supposed to be one of the first houses built in the town. And the fact that it had been a Speakeasy meant that there were probably lots of stories it could tell. Of course, Molly had been here during those days so, she probably had a lot of stories to tell, too. James, however, didn't like to think about that part of her past. She was a wonderful woman and the light of his life. That's all he needed to know about that part of her life.

Molly had refreshed his lemonade, and they went back out to the porch. "I don't know why that startled me so," said Molly.

"It had just been so peaceful sitting here together. That's all," said James. He took her hand and rocked both chairs together for a time.

The next sound they heard was the boys coming to look at the stairs and what Maxwell had planned. Ordinarily, they would be using the back stairs to head up at night, though tonight, Maxwell wanted to share his vision, and everyone was mildly interested. At least they all pretended to be.

James stepped in, and everyone got quiet. "You left the tape measure at the top of the stairs, and it fell to the floor and startled Miss Molly a few minutes ago," said James to Maxwell. Maxwell didn't want to argue, but he knew he had left everything at the bottom of the stairs.

"Sorry," said Maxwell.

"Just be more careful with your tools next time," said James. "I don't want any tools left on the staircase, ever." He was adamant.

Curious, thought Maxwell. *That's twice today that something unexplainable has happened on that staircase, and the boys had told him someone was murdered there. Was the stairwell haunted?*

James said goodnight and went back out on the porch with Molly. She was watching two birds settle into the Elm tree in the front yard. She thought they were Mockingbirds, but in the twilight, it was hard to tell for sure. She asked James what he thought, but James' eyes hadn't adjusted to the light. He didn't even see them.

Fall was in the air, and the breeze felt wonderful. The summer had been exceptionally hot. Some folks were saying the winter would be very cold. For now, it was Fall and most enjoyable.

They watched a horse-drawn carriage stroll down the street headed for downtown. It was probably a couple going to the theater. There was still some money left in the county, and there were Ranchers and Oilmen who could afford the theater and a nice dinner in town.

Molly waved, but the couple acted as if they weren't there. Molly took no notice and turned to

James, "We should go to the theater soon. Don't you think that would be fun?"

"Yes," he said. "Let me know when you want to go. I'll make all the arrangements." Meaning he would buy the tickets for the seats around them so that Molly would not have to listen to the rude remarks of some of the "upper crust" patrons about the "lady of the evening." James tried to shield Molly from their mean attitudes whenever he could.

James yawned, and Molly took that as a sign he was ready to go to bed. "Shall we go inside?" she asked.

"That sounds good," said James. "I want to start early in the morning. We're running freshwater to the apartment tomorrow."

Molly took James's hand and led him into the house. Maxwell was sitting at the bottom of the stairs with his head in his hands.

"What's wrong, boy?" asked James.

"I don't understand. I marked several of the spindles where I planned to hand carve birds. The marks are all gone. They're just gone like I never marked them," said Maxwell.

"Show me where you had them marked," said James.

"I don't remember exactly," said Maxwell. "I made notes in this pad that Miss Molly gave me, but I don't find any marks on the spindles anywhere."

"That doesn't make any sense," said James.

"Oh, strange things happen on that staircase," said Molly. "Wouldn't surprise me at all if something erased your marks. Just be sure to write things in your notepad."

James and Maxwell just stared at her. She was serious. She wasn't frightened at all by what she was saying. She was describing some kind of magical staircase as if it were perfectly normal.

"Molly, does that not seem a bit odd to you?" questioned James.

"It's an odd staircase, James. I didn't make it that way. I just know that it is that way," she said as if it made perfect sense. "You can't question every little strange thing that happens in a house this old. You'll go crazy."

James and Maxwell exchanged looks, shook their heads, and turned to go. Maxwell was starting to understand why there had been a vacancy.

The next morning at breakfast, after Molly had sat down to eat, she said, "Maxwell, those markings are on the stairs. It must have just been a trick of the light last night made them look like they had disappeared."

To everyone's surprise, Maxwell and James bolted out of the room towards the entry. The markings were back.

"Well, that's mighty queer," said James. "Did we imagine it?"

"I don't think so, sir," said Maxwell. "You mind if I start carving on this today? You know, before anything else disappears."

"Sounds like a solid plan to me, boy. Let's go finish breakfast. Then you can get started. You need a helper to dismantle it?"

"Only for a little bit, I can come to get someone when I'm ready."

"Good enough," said James as they walked back in to breakfast.

"Where's Andy?" asked James as he sat down.

"He cleared out, Mr. Thacker," said Billy. "He got scared about the house being haunted."

"Oh, for the love of Pete!" yelled James. "Enough breakfast. Let's go get some work done." He stormed out the back door. Everyone except Maxwell followed him.

"Are you quitting, too?" asked Miss Molly.

"No, Ma'am. I'm working on the staircase today."

"Oh, good. I'll check on you from time to time to make sure the haint didn't get you." She giggled as she said it.

"Haint?" said Maxwell.

"That's what some folks call them. You probably call them ghosts. Some folks call them Haints." Miss Molly explained.

"Did you tell the boys about what happened on the staircase last night?" said Maxwell.

"Why, yes. They wanted to know why you and Mr. Thacker jumped up from the table like that, so I told them."

"They don't frighten you at all, do they?" asked Maxwell.

"Who?" asked Miss Molly.

"The Haints," said Maxwell.

"Oh, sweetie, they been here forever. They don't mean any real harm most of the time. They just like to prank people," she answered nonchalantly.

"So, you told the boys at breakfast that there was a ghost here?" he asked.

"They asked what was going on. I told them. I better get started on these dishes. They're not going to clean themselves, and I've never heard of a haint doing dishes."

Maxwell mulled this new information over in his mind while he worked at disassembling the staircase. *I guess it's time for me to decide if I believe in ghosts,* he thought. *And then I'll need to decide if I'm afraid of them.*

The banister came loose pretty easy, but he had to go get help to lift it off and carry it out to the shop. No one wanted to volunteer, so James assigned the job to Earl.

"You're not afraid to work on this?" asked Earl as they were lifting up the baluster.

"Nah. It hasn't done me any harm. It's like working with someone who has a keen sense of humor." Maxwell answered.

"What if something decides to push you off from the top like they did that guy that died here a few years ago? Doesn't that idea scare ya'? You shouldn't be working on this in here by yourself. There's safety in numbers."

"You volunteering?" joked Maxwell.

"Shoot, no," said Earl. "But the boss wouldn't care if you asked for help."

"Thanks, Earl. I'll think about it."

The two men lifted the banister and carefully relocated it to the shop out back. Maxwell would try to do most of the carving out there. He went back in to begin the long slow process of unscrewing each spindle. He numbered them as he went so that the whole thing would go back together easily. He made sure to **carve** the number in the bottom of each spindle. No more trickster haints erasing marks and messing with that part of the project.

The disassembly took most of the day. Meanwhile, the rest of the boys were working on the freshwater to the second apartment. They finished before Maxwell did and were out back having a beer when he finally carried his last load of spindles out to the shop. He still needed to put up a safety railing, and that would require help.

"Earl, I'm going to need your help again here in a few minutes," he called out to Earl.

"Glad to oblige," said Earl.

Off they went with a long two-by-four to tack a railing in place and call it a day.

Maxwell joined the crew on the back porch, and Miss Molly brought him a beer before he could ask. James had taken Ted home by way of the pub, so he would be gone until dinner time.

Miss Molly lingered to visit with the crew for a few minutes. She enjoyed socializing and had very few opportunities for it anymore.

"Did the haint leave you alone today?" she asked Maxwell bluntly.

"Didn't see any sign of it," he replied. "And I'll be working in the shop now on all the parts."

"Well, I'll miss having company in the house," she said with a wink.

As soon as she left, the questions started:

"What's a haint?"

"Is there something going on between you two?"

"Aren't you afraid of the big guy finding out?"

"Are you crazy? Flirting with the boss's wife?"

"A haint is a ghost," said Maxwell.

"Nothing is going on between us. I don't know what she's talking about. She never said a word to me while I was working inside. And, you'll notice, I wasn't flirting with her."

"Boss won't care who was doing the flirting if he catches her flirting with you, he's going to think you brought it on."

"Well, I can't exactly stop her. Besides, she flirts with everyone."

"Who does?" said James as he walked up from the side yard.

"Didn't see you there, Mr. Thacker," said Maxwell. "I got all the spindles in the garage, and I'm ready to start spinning them," he said, trying to change the subject.

"Okay, good. I'll fetch the lathe over tomorrow," said Mr. Thacker.

Maxwell smiled. It worked!

"Now who's this flirt ya'll are talking about?"

Maxwell gave Mr. Thacker a blank stare.

"Oh, just a shop-girl in town," said Maxwell.

"I see," said Mr. Thacker, "because I thought you might be talking about my wife." He said without breaking a smile.

No one said a word. The air was heavy with anticipation of what Maxwell would say next.

"Your wife is a beautiful woman, and many a man would mistake that smile for a flirtation if they did not know her to be married," said Maxwell. "But I can assure you that we were not discussing your wife, Mr. Thacker."

Mr. Thacker burst out laughing, "Maxwell, my wife, is the biggest flirt in this town. She misses the days when this old house was a speakeasy, and she was a hostess of gay parties every night of the week. Of **course,** you were talking about her."

Maxwell was not reassured by Mr. Thacker's manner. He felt that this was not a good direction for the conversation to go.

"Mr. Thacker, your wife is indeed very friendly, but I would not for one-minute mistake that friendliness for flirtation," said Maxwell.

"Then why did you say she was a flirt with everyone?" asked Mr. Thacker. He was no longer laughing.

"I honestly don't remember what I said exactly, Mr. Thacker, but whatever it was, I assure you, I didn't mean any offense by it."

"Watch yourself, boy," said Mr. Thacker as he walked on into the house. "I got my eye on you."

There was no conversation for a long time. Everyone just sat there, sipping their beers, and looking around the yard. If there was a part of that property that needed attention, it was duly noted during that long silence.

"I reckon I'm going to go wash up for dinner," said Billy.

The others followed in silence. Maxwell brought up the rear and wished he could take the whole conversation back. This was a nice house with nice people, and he had been looking forward to being here for a long time. Now it looked like that might not be the case. Mr. Thacker seemed pretty upset about the whole thing. Maxwell wasn't looking forward to dinner.

The bell rang for dinner. The crew filed down the back stairs single file to the kitchen table. Mr. Thacker was already sitting at the table. Mrs. Thacker was her usual smiling, animated self. The boys took their seats and waited for Mr. Thacker to signal it was okay to start loading up their plates. He just sat there. He waited until Mrs. Thacker had taken her seat. They had never seen him do this before, and it left everyone a bit confused.

"Dig in, boys," he said.

The ice was broken, and the meal began in earnest. Bowls were passed, and questions were asked. Miss Molly told everyone about the visitor she had had that day. It was a salesman, but she didn't care. She was excited to have a visitor. James joined in the conversation as if nothing had happened. But he did seem to have thought about the way he set the example for how to treat his wife.

Maxwell noticed that there was some kind of biscuit on Mr. Thacker's plate that no one else had. Molly saw him notice and winked at him like they shared a secret. She must have made something special for Mr. Thacker. She was such a sweet woman. He probably would do more than flirt with her if it weren't for Mr. Thacker.

After everyone had finished up, James and Molly went out to the front porch.

"Let's take a walk," said Molly. "I'd like to walk around the courthouse square."

James didn't mind, so they started strolling toward the courthouse. It was only two or three blocks away, and it was a pleasant evening for a walk. By the time they reached the courthouse, James was having stomach cramps.

"I think we need to go back to the house," he said to Molly.

"Whatever for?" she asked. "It's lovely out tonight."

"I'm not feeling well," said James. "I need to get back to the house."

"Oh, my," said Molly. "Should we take a taxi?"

"Yes, yes. Let's hail a cab," he was hurting bad now.

He hailed a cab, and they were home in minutes. "Boys!" he called out from the entry. He needed help to get to the bedroom. He had already tried to relieve himself to no avail. He now felt as though he was going to lose his dinner. And the cramping was becoming unbearable.

Molly stood there, watching. Her usual smile had been replaced with a grin that could have belonged to a clown. It was almost evil. The boys came running in.

They all shouted various versions of "What's going on?"

Molly just stood there as if in shock. "I don't know," she said innocently. "He started having stomach pains when we were out walking. Now he can't even stand up. He threw up once already. I don't know what to do to help him. Will you help me get him into bed?"

They picked the big man up to carry him. He moaned even louder as they straightened him out.

"Leave me here. It hurts too much to straighten out."

Molly sent one of the boys to fetch the Dr.

James lay there, moaning and occasionally screaming from the pain.

"Maybe some whiskey would help," offered Billy.

"I'll take some," moaned James.

Billy ran to fetch it. The Doctor rushed in asking questions.

"When did it start? What did he have to eat today? Why isn't he in a bed? Whose idea was it to give him whiskey?"

"It started about half an hour ago while we were taking an evening stroll downtown. He was hurting so bad we had to take a taxi home. He ate what we all ate for dinner. We had chicken and potatoes and corn and biscuits and gravy. He won't let us carry him to bed. Billy suggested whiskey," said Molly.

"You all ate the same meal, but he's the only one hurting?" asked the Dr.

"Well," Maxwell started to tell him about the biscuit, but Molly shot him a look, and instead, he said, "My stomach was a little off a while ago, but I'm fine now."

Miss Molly smiled at him and nodded. Maxwell didn't like how this was looking. Had Miss Molly poisoned her husband? She just didn't seem like the type.

"Well, I need him in a bed if I'm going to examine him," said Dr. Sparks. "Give me a hand, boys. He may not like it, but it has to be done."

Mr. Thacker screamed and fought them as they lifted him up to move him to the bedroom. But the Dr. was insistent that he should be in a bed. It took all of them, but they got him in there. His stomach was swollen. He was a big man, but his stomach looked like he'd swallowed a big balloon. No wonder he had belched a couple of times while they were moving him.

The doctor shooed everyone out except Mrs. Thacker. "Mrs. Thacker, we need to get these clothes off of him. I think it will make him feel better. I'm going to roll him. You do the tugging. We'll get the pants off first."

"What do you think is wrong, Doc?" asked Mrs. Thacker. "Is he going to be okay?"

"It's hard to say. It doesn't look like food poisoning, though. We may just have to ride it out and see what happens. Get one of the boys to bring me some charcoal."

Mrs. Thacker left the room. The boys were all just outside the door. Before she could speak, someone said, "Billy's gone to find some charcoal." Everyone was worried and wanting to be helpful.

Molly went back into the bedroom. James was screaming and moaning and clutching his stomach. "Can't you give him something for the pain, Doc?" she pleaded.

The Doctor withdrew a needle from his bag. "This will get rid of the pain, but it won't help us determine what is causing it."

"Just give it to me, Doc. I can't take this much longer."

The Doctor injected him with morphine, which calmed him immediately and lulled the man into a fitful sleep.

"That's all I can do for now," he said. "Send for me if anything changes. I will be at my house all day, or they will know where I am."

"Thank you, Dr.," said Mrs. Thacker. "What if he wakes up in pain again?"

"He won't wake up from that for hours. I'll stop back in before that."

"I'll keep an eye on him just in case," she said.

She showed the Dr. to the door and asked Billy to take the first watch sitting with Mr. Thacker. She excused herself to the kitchen and found a bottle of whiskey. She drank a shot. This was a level of nervous she had never experienced before. It looked like she was going to get away with it. All this time pretending she was happy living with a house full of men that she could only barely flirt with. It drove her crazy. Her husband did not understand.

But the traveling salesman this afternoon had understood only too well. And he had had a solution. He had sold her a potion that would get rid of her husband once and for all. She had used it in a special biscuit just for him.

The deed was done with no one the wiser, with the possible exception of that handsome young Maxwell. He had noticed. He spotted it at the dinner table and almost spilled the beans to the Doc. Could she trust him? She didn't want to use any more of the potion. It would be too coincidental. And besides, she liked Maxwell. She hoped he would stay on. She wanted to get to know him better.

Billy came out of the bedroom, "Mrs. Thacker, his breathing isn't good. He almost isn't breathing at all."

"Run, fetch the Dr.," she said.

"She hurried into the bedroom. James was a fine-looking man. She was beginning to think maybe she should have let things be. She really liked him and couldn't think of a reason to get rid of him. She looked up and saw a man dressed in clown face sitting on the other side of the bed.

"Why are you here now? I need you to leave me in peace," she said in horror.

The man in the mask just looked at her, and her mind lapsed back into being thankful that the potion was working, and her husband would soon be dead, and no one would know it was her.

As the Doctor came in, Molly moved aside to give him room to check James's vital signs.

"This could just be his reaction to the morphine. It is slowing his system down, but I would not have expected it to slow down this much. This is not a good sign, Mrs. Thacker," he said as gently as he could. "I will stay for half an hour and see if this condition improves."

"Thank you, Doctor. I don't know what to do to help him," she said.

"There is nothing you can do now. If you believe in prayer, that is the only thing left to do."

Mrs. Thacker went out into the hall, where the boys were gathered. "It's time to pray, boys. That's all that's left to be done. The Dr. doesn't know what it is, but he knows it doesn't look good."

She went back into the bedroom to wait with the Dr. She knew better than anyone that it was just a matter of time. The clown was in the room, leaning on the mantle. He always made her feel calmer about what was going on. She remembered the first day he showed up. She was still a "working girl" in this very house. He never spoke, but whenever he was there, she seemed to know exactly what needed to be done. It felt good.

Sometimes he would be in the house for days at a time, and other times, he would stay gone for months. She wasn't sure why he showed up, but something mysterious usually happened shortly after he did.

This time he had shown up just before the traveling salesman. It was a funny thing. Molly didn't remember being unhappy with James before. Now it felt like she had always been unhappy. She wished she had never seen the clown. She wished the traveling salesman had not stopped at her house.

James had no son, so the house would be hers now. She wondered if the crew would stay on. She wondered if the clown would let her be. She heard a commotion upstairs. She went to the door to see what was going on. Maxwell had slipped near the temporary top railing of the front staircase. He was okay but shaken.

She went back to the bedroom. The clown looked at her and raised his clown eyebrows as if to say, "The staircase is an issue."

"He's gone," whispered the Dr. "He has stopped breathing."

"James, no. Don't leave me. I can't do this without you. I need you." All the love came pouring back in. She didn't cry at first. She held him and begged him for twenty minutes, not to go. The Dr. left her in the room to come to terms with what had happened. The clown appeared and jumped around the room clapping. Molly was horrified. She finally burst into tears.

The Dr. came in and pulled her up and away from the bed. He poured the poor woman a shot of whiskey, urging her to drink it down. She had lost control, and the tears were flowing.

"I'll send one of the boys for the mortician," he said as he left the room again. It seemed to take only minutes for him to get there, but in reality, it had taken an hour. Time meant nothing to Molly right now. She refused to let go of James. The mortician finally pried her hand free and started to prepare the body to be moved.

The Dr. gave her a sedative to help her sleep that night. He told Billy that he would come around first thing in the morning to check on her.

As she fell asleep, she whispered to Billy, "Get Maxwell to put the staircase back the way it was."

"We can take care of that later, Miss Molly. Don't you worry about anything right now. We're here for you," he said, thinking she was just rambling.

"NO," she shouted. "Put it back like it was! Do it immediately." Then her voice trailed off as she muttered something about a clown and an accident.

She awoke the next morning to the Doctor, checking her head and her pulse. "You seem to be calmer this morning, Mrs. Thacker. That was a pretty strong sedative I gave you last night."

"Where am I?" she asked. "Am I in a hospital?" She looked around the room and her vision cleared enough to see she was in her own room.

She started to scream when she saw the clown was still there. "I slept in the bed where he just died?" she yelled. "You left me here alone with his spirit and the clown?"

Dr. Sparks injected her with a sedative. "She is in shock over the sudden loss of her husband. She will need to be watched. Can you men take turns sitting with her?"

"Of course," said Billy. We'll keep an eye on her, sir."

"I'll send one of the ladies from the church over to help, and I'll be back in a few hours to look in on her," said the Dr. "What was she yelling about a clown?"

"I don't know, Sir. She said we needed to put the stairs back right and keep an eye out for the clown."

"She may be hallucinating from the medication I gave her," said the doctor. "Just keep an eye on her."

Around mid-day, the doctor came back with an older woman. "This is Mrs. White. She is my housekeeper, but for the next day or two, she will be helping out here. Mind her orders, and we will get Mrs. Thacker back to a good state of mind and health."

"Show me the kitchen, Billy," said Mrs. White. "We'll need some tea and some broth. I'm assuming you men can fend for yourselves for food." It wasn't a question so much as a statement.

Billy showed her to the kitchen. The boys had already eaten and cleaned up the mess. Mrs. White put on a kettle for tea and looked in the icebox for broth or broth makings. She found what she needed and set to work.

Billy went upstairs with the rest of the crew. "She was pretty angry about them stairs not being put back. Maybe we should work on that today," he said to no one in particular.

"It might make some noise. Maybe we should work on something outside."

"Why should we work on anything," said another. "The boss is dead, and his wife is looking kind of crazy. We may not even have a job anymore."

"As long as we have a room to stay in and food to eat, we owe a day's work," said Maxwell. "If we're quiet, we can get all the stair parts back in the house, and I can put them back together pretty quiet."

"It's as good a thing to do as any, I guess," said Billy.

It made them all feel better to be doing something. As they started carrying in the spindles, Mrs. White poked her head out the door to tell them to shush. They started tiptoeing and laying the pieces down one at a time. She nodded approval and slipped back into the bedroom with Mrs. Thacker.

This time when Mrs. Thacker woke up, Mrs. White was sitting there with some tea. Mrs. Thacker was still woozy from the sedative, but she understood where she was this time. She did not, however, recognize Mrs. White. And, to her delight, the clown was nowhere to be seen.

"Have some tea, dear. Are you hungry? I have some biscuits here and some broth."

"No, tea will be fine," Mrs. Thacker all but whispered. "Where is my husband?"

Mrs. White sighed and started to tell Mrs. Thacker what had happened when Mrs. Thacker interrupted.

"I understand that he is dead, but where is he? He was lying in this bed. Where is he now?"

"He is at the funeral parlor. There was some concern about the manner of his death, but the doctor examined him and determined it was some form of food poisoning, so he is being prepared for burial."

Mrs. Thacker looked across the room. There was the clown, once again leaning against the mantle. He pointed to the upstairs.

"The stairs," said Mrs. Thacker. "Are the stairs being put back right?

"Yes," said Mrs. White. "I tried to get them to hold off. We didn't want to wake you, but they insisted that you wanted this done immediately."

"I do," said Mrs. Thacker. "I have reason to believe there will be an accident on that stairway if it is not repaired quickly. Do not ask me why I know it. I just know."

"Calm yourself," said Mrs. White. "It's being taken care of. The boys seemed happy to be doing something that you wanted to be done."

"Happy? How can anyone be happy when my poor James is dead?" cried Mrs. Thacker.

"Oh, there, there," said Mrs. White as she petted the new widow's hand. "I didn't mean happy, so much as less sad. It's easier to get through something like this if you can keep yourself busy. Do you have any needlepoint or cross-stitch to work on that I can get for you?"

"No, I never learned to stitch like that," said Mrs. Thacker.

"Dear me. What do you do with yourself all day?" said Mrs. White.

"I take care of this house." The clown was back, and Molly knew just what to do.

"All these men and not one woman to help with the housework? That's just not right. I can help you find someone if you like."

Maybe Mrs. White wasn't judging her after all. Maybe she didn't know what to do. The clown pointed upstairs.

"Mrs. White, would you mind going to the top of the stairs to fetch me a book? I'm sure it's in the bookcase at the top of the stairs. It's called Pride and Prejudice. It might be a good book for me right now."

"I'll go fetch it now," said Mrs. White. She disappeared as did the clown.

Within minutes Molly heard a crash. There was a great deal of commotion in the entry. Molly still felt faint from the sedative. She tried to get up to see what had happened, but she fell to the floor. She screamed out for Billy.

Billy had sent for the Dr. when he heard Miss Molly scream. He ran in to find her on the floor. He helped her up and tried to get her into bed. She fought him.

"I want to see what is going on out there," she said.

"There's been an accident, Mrs. Thacker. I've sent for the doctor. I think we may have lost Maxwell. Mrs. White seems to be breathing still."

Looking up at the fractured stairwell, there stood the clown. The laughter pierced her ears. She screamed. Billy assumed it was the sight of Maxwell with a sharp piece of wood sticking up through his chest or the sight of Mrs. White, who had landed on top of him. He guided her back into the bedroom and let her sit on the side of the bed until she finally laid down of her own accord.

The doctor rushed in and assessed the situation quickly. There was nothing to be done for Maxwell. A wood shard had pierced his heart. Mrs. White would be sore, but a careful examination revealed no broken bones. She would survive.

"Help me move her to the sofa," called Dr. Sparks. "Did anyone see what happened?"

"She went up there to get a book, and Maxwell was stooped over attaching some spindles. They were the only two up there. She fell forward like she tripped. That knocked Maxwell over the edge then she just fell on top of him. It probably wouldn't have happened if the banister had been connected in place." This was Joe's account.

"All I saw was both of them falling," said Earl.

"He's dead, ain't he?" said Billy.

"Yes, yes, he is. We'll need to get the police over here. Send someone to fetch them, will you?" The Dr. said to Billy.

"I'll go myself," said Billy. "I could use the fresh air."

The Dr. looked around at the mess. He had told the police that James had died from food poisoning even though he knew it wasn't. He wasn't sure what it was, but it wasn't food poisoning. He knew their situation and knew Molly didn't need a police investigation. Her mind was fragile. Better to believe it was food poisoning than go through a long investigation and trial about it.

But he couldn't cover this up. It would be ruled accidental, of course. But how would Molly react? Would this be what pushed her permanently over the edge? All this talk of a clown wasn't going to help her situation. She was talking about it even now. She had been telling Billy that a clown had pushed Mrs. White over that stairway.

"Don't tell a soul she said that," said Dr. Sparks to Billy. "That stays between you and me. It's the sedative I gave her. Nothing more."

But the good doctor knew there **was** something more going on. He wasn't sure what, but there was **something**. He had been to this house before when people had seen a clown in the hours before someone mysteriously died. Was it a ghost? No one found out then. He doubted that anyone would find out now.

Mrs. Thacker would clearly need time in a hospital. There was a mental hospital not far from the house. He would have her admitted for a few weeks of rest and grief counseling.

It would take that long for the paperwork to be sorted out regarding the estate of Mr. Thacker. But it was well known that there was enough money there to pay for Mrs. Thacker's recuperation time. Dr. Sparks could even see himself courting her. This was a lovely house. He would not mind owning it after a suitable waiting period when he proposed to Mrs. Thacker. He knew she would say yes.

The late Maxwell leaned against the wall at the top of the staircase, watching the scene with a hint of detached amusement. He was almost expressionless with his arms folded in front of him, and his old cowboy hat tilted slightly on his head. He didn't seem to notice the clown.

But the clown was there, laughing, standing at the spot where he had pushed Mrs. White through the stairs.

The clown welcomed the opportunity to cause more mischief. He had all the time in the world to wait for the next show. Maybe he would accompany Mrs. Thacker to the hospital. He was becoming quite attached to her.

The End?

Story 8

Louise and Margie

Louise and Margie were excited about the New Year's Eve Party they were hosting this year. They had been preparing for it for weeks. They had invited the other residents of the triplex they lived in and also the local neighbors so there wouldn't be any complaints. They had prepared an h'orderves list, and there would be finger sandwiches and a spiked punch bowl. Margie had found a picture in a fashion magazine of a party tray with the cheeses arranged in the shape of a New Year's Hat with the band consisting of the crackers. She was sure she could copy it easily.

The day after Christmas, they started getting the rooms ready for the party. They rearranged the living room and the bedroom so both could be used for socializing. The week was spent getting everything perfect. They both knew

199

this was going to be a smashing welcome to the year nineteen-forty.

"Are you sure you'll be able to make the radish garnish look like little roses?" Louise asked Margie.

"I made them once for a party my mother was having. They were beautiful," said Margie. "Did you pick up the colored toothpicks?"

"I did. The store had some delightful paper napkins with pictures of Martinis on them, so I bought some of those, too."

"We're not going over budget, are we?" questioned Margie.

"Oh, what if we do? Who cares? This is going to be the best New Year's Eve party ever!" Louise could barely contain her excitement.

"I care," said Margie. "We still have to pay the rent on the second."

"I've held out the rent money," said Louise. "It's in an envelope in my top drawer. I won't touch that. And we'll have oodles of leftover food to get us through the first couple of weeks. Then we get paid again!"

"How much do we have left for the last-minute items?" asked Margie.

"Last minute like what?" asked Louise.

"Like vegetables, and cream and little things we might have forgotten," said Margie in a more or less irritated tone.

"I already picked up the vegetables and the cream and the Sherbet for the punch and the fruits and nuts. I think we have everything checked off the list we made."

"Let me see," said Margie. She studied the list just knowing Louise would have forgotten something, but it looked complete. "Looks like you've done a good job, Louise. Well done!" But something was nagging at her. She could feel it in her bones that they forgot something important.

"Champagne!" she shouted. "We don't have champagne! Quick! How much money do we have? A good bottle of Champagne will be at least two dollars, and we may need more than one!" Margie was in a panic.

Louise walked into the kitchen and walked back out with a bottle of champagne. "You mean like this?" she said, smiling. Louise was so proud of herself.

"Oh, Louise, how could I doubt you? Of course, you thought of everything. Even what wasn't on our list."

Margie looked around at the living room and thought about what it would be like in a couple more nights with dozens of people enjoying the music and the food and the drinks. They had borrowed a record player from the couple downstairs, and they had told all their friends to bring a record. It was going to be perfect.

"My mother gave me a new blouse for Christmas. I'm going to wear it for the party," said Louise.

"I don't have anything new," said Margie, "but I have something nice."

"Show me," said Louise. "I'd love to see it. I may have something to add to it, so it will look new."

Margie went to the closet and brought out a light blue chiffon dress. It had a silk scarf for a belt, and there were dark blue sequins around the neckline.

"That is beautiful!" said Louise. "I wouldn't change a thing about it. It looks very fashionable and up to date."

"Thank you," said Margie. "I know it's not that up to date, but it is pretty, isn't it?"

"Yes, it is. It looks lovely," said Louise.

Neither of them remembered a time when the country wasn't in a depression, but the news of the day was that it was over and things were going to be much better now. They both had found work in town after graduating from High School, and that was a good sign. They had seen this charming apartment house with a vacancy they could afford. That was another good sign. In fact, the apartment was less than they would have expected for such a lovely space. The year nineteen-forty was looking good for both of them.

Louise even had a boy calling on her. Her father didn't like the idea of her receiving gentleman callers at an apartment and insisted she receive him at their home. But Louise didn't tell him everything.

Margie hadn't met the right one yet, but she went out on double dates with Louise. Louise's father didn't mind her going on double dates from the apartment. Well, he may have cared just a little, but he had given his permission. Margie enjoyed the outings and always looked forward to them. They had both decided not to have a male partner for their party, though. They would need to devote all their attention to playing hostesses.

It was getting late, and they both had to work the next day. They decided to go to bed and read for a bit. Their bedroom had two twin beds, each with a nightstand and a lamp. They shared a closet. They had moved the beds to the side of the room and brought in some folding chairs. They would make them look like daybeds for the party.

Louise was reading a new romance novel, and Margie was reading something about Winning Friends and Influencing People. She thought she could use all the help she could get, and this was supposed to be the best self-help book there was.

Louise drifted off to sleep, so Margie ended up having to turn both their lights out. At that point, she realized there was a light on in the living room. *Drat*, she thought, *I hate having to go out there at night. It's too creepy with all the windows.* She got up and put on her night robe. She walked into the living room to find there was no light on. As she looked toward the bathroom, she saw a ball of light. It seemed to be hovering about waist level in the doorway. Then it began to move back and forth across the doorway. Then it disappeared.

Margie gasped. "Who is there?" she called. "What are you doing? What game is this?"

No one responded. Margie felt a chill run up her spine. The hair on the back of her neck prickled up and tingled. She backed slowly out of the living room and back towards the bedroom. She slept with the light on that night.

The next morning at breakfast, she asked Louise, "Have you ever noticed a strange light in the living room or the bathroom?"

"What kind of light?" said Louise. "Like the moonlight coming through the skylight?"

"No, more like a lightning bug only a hundred times bigger," said Margie.

"That's not even possible," said Louise. "You were dreaming. Probably because you fell asleep with your light on, so you dreamed of a light."

"But it wasn't a dream. I saw it before I went to sleep. It was so bright I thought we had left a light on in the living room. I went in to turn it off. That's when I saw it," said Margie.

"You were dreaming," insisted Louise. "Now let's shake a leg. We're going to be late for work. One more night until the party!" she reminded Margie.

Margie knew it hadn't been a dream. She didn't care what Louise said. She knew what she had seen with her own eyes. It was a giant ball of light drifting through the air alone. *What could it have been?* She thought.

Neither Margie nor Louise had a car yet, so they walked to work. They each worked in opposite directions from the house. They walked together for half a block, then parted ways.

"See you tonight," called Louise.

"Okie dokie," called Margie.

They had brought sandwiches for lunch. Louise would eat hers in a back room of the dress shop where she worked as a sales clerk. Margie would eat hers at her desk in the newspaper office where she answered the phone and helped people place want ads. She had found she was quite good at writing the ads.

During the day, she talked to one of the reporters, "Have you ever heard of a floating ball of light just appearing in someone's room?"

"Sounds a lot like one of those Science Fiction writers," he said. "Are you trying to get into the Science Fiction writing business? You won't get any work here. People around here don't like to read about that stuff."

"So, you don't believe it could happen?" she asked.

"Maybe I do, and maybe I don't, but I wouldn't go admitting it to anyone around this town if I did. Catch my drift?" said the reporter raising his eyebrows as if conveying a code.

"Not really," said Margie. "I saw one last night with my own eyes. It was in my living room."

"No kidding?" said Mr. Flaherty, the reporter. "Take some advice and don't be telling anybody else about it. They'll be locking you in the mental home with talk like that."

"I won't mention it to anyone else but you," said Margie.

"Smart girl," said Mr. Flaherty.

Margie went back to her desk and finished out the day without mentioning the strange blue light to anyone else.

Louise was already home when Margie arrived. "Did you have a good day?" asked Margie.

"I sold two dresses and a hat and three belts," said Louise. "I'm so glad to be on commission now."

"That sounds great," said Margie. "I was wondering. Would it be okay if I invited someone from the newspaper to the party tomorrow night? He probably wouldn't come, but I'd like to ask him."

"I don't see why not," said Louise. "We have plenty of food and beverages."

"Good. I'll ask him in the morning." Margie was smiling.

They fixed some dinner together and decided to go for a walk to "window shop." They were both too excited to sleep yet. They talked about their days and about some of the new outfits in the storefronts. Louise was keen on a new shade of blue that seemed to be the fashion this year. Margie was less colorful and didn't think as much about clothing styles. She was happy with a black skirt and a white shirt most of the time.

The sun went down, causing the air to become chilly. They headed back to the apartment. They stopped off and visited with the downstairs neighbors and finally went on up to their flat. They both had to work the next day, which was New Year's Eve, but Louise had the New Year's Day off, and Margie didn't have to go in until eleven. They curled each other's hair and eased into bed.

Once again, Louise fell asleep with the light on. Margie turned it off for her, but as she rolled over to turn her light out, she noticed a light coming from the bathroom. She got up and shook Louise. "Shhhh. Get up and come with me," she said to Louise.

"Why? What is wrong?"

"Just be quiet and follow me," whispered Margie.

There it was in the bathroom. It was floating near the same doorway between the bathroom and the living room.

"Do you see it now?" whispered Margie.

Louise looked and saw it for the first time. She stared for a minute, then she let out a scream.

"Shhhhh. Shush," said Margie, but it was too late. The blue light was gone.

Louise's scream had unnerved Margie for a minute. She was shaking. Louise was not screaming anymore, but now she was gasping.

"What was that?" Louise yelled.

"I don't know," said Margie. "That's why I wanted you to see it, too. It wasn't a dream, and it's not my imagination. You saw it, too."

"We need to move. We need to move now!" yelled Louise.

"Calm down, please," said Margie. "I need to think. I need to do some research. I can find out what's going on. We don't need to move."

"I'm not staying here," yelled Louise. "It's not safe. What was that?"

"Let's go back to the bedroom and think about it," whispered Margie trying to calm Louise down.

She led Louise back to bed and gave her some paregoric to help her sleep. It put her right out and left Margie alone to sort through what she knew. She knew she wasn't crazy. She had a witness. She knew, so far, the ball of light had stayed in the same area. She knew screaming tended to scare it away. She would talk to Mr.

Flaherty tomorrow. He would know how to investigate this. He was in his twenties's and a seasoned reporter, after all.

Margie didn't sleep well that night. She was glad to see the sunrise and quickly woke Louise.

"I had the strangest dream last night," said Louise. "You woke me up to show me your strange ball of light. It scared me, and I screamed. That's all I remember. I wish you'd stop telling me your stories. I don't like that kind of dream."

Margie started to tell her the truth but decided it was best to leave it alone. At least this way, she wasn't going on about needing to move.

They both dressed and left for work. Margie couldn't wait to see Mr. Flaherty. Her witness didn't remember, but she had a witness now. She made it to her desk early and watched for him to come in then jumped up to meet him at his station when he arrived.

"It happened again last night. This time my roommate saw it, too," she blurted out.

"Shhhh. What did I tell you about talking about that around here? Keep your voice down," he said as he grabbed her arm and forced her to sit down at his desk.

Margie started to whisper, "Louise saw the blue light, too, last night. She doesn't remember it, but only because I gave her paregoric to put her to sleep. She saw it. It scared her so much she screamed."

"You drugged your roommate, then she saw your mysterious light?" he asked. "I don't see how that helps your case."

"She saw the light before I drugged her. Wait. I didn't drug her. I just gave her something to calm her down. It worked."

"We don't need to be talking about this here. Let's have lunch in the park where no one is listening," he said.

"Okay," she said. "Listen, we're having a New Year's Eve party at our place tonight. Would you like to come? There'll be food, music, people, and spiked punch, and we even have a bottle of champagne for midnight."

"Maybe," he said. "I'll have to check my calendar. I forgot it was New Year's Eve."

He laughed and then said, "Sure, I'll come. What's the address?"

She wrote down the address and said, "I'll see you at lunch," as she walked away.

They drove the few blocks to the park in his car. They found a beautiful sunny spot away from everyone.

"So, what do you think you have? An alien? A ghost? A spirit? A faery?"

"I don't know what to think, but it's appeared two nights in a row that I know of. It's not a coincidence. It doesn't feel like an alien, and I don't know what a ghost or a fairy looks like."

"Slow down. You're making me dizzy, and you're talking so fast. You said it's like a ball, right?"

Margie nodded.

"Can you see through it?

"Sort of. Like the way you can see through a light bulb."

"And it floats?"

She nodded again.

"Up and down or side to side?"

"Both," she said.

"I'll look into it. Maybe there's been some stories written about such things. Let me do some digging."

"That would be great," she said.

"We better get back to the office," he said. They drove back in silence, but it wasn't uncomfortable.

Margie managed to slip out of work two hours early. She went straight to the house and started setting things up for the party. They had told people to arrive at about eight, so no one would feel rushed after work, and no one would think it was a dinner party. Margie decided she had enough time to put her hair up in curlers for an hour to freshen up her "do."

She was in very high spirits as she now had someone taking this anomaly seriously, and she didn't feel crazy. Louise arrived home an hour early and stopped to put her hair up in curlers, too. She then pitched in with getting the h'orderves ready. They put on a record album and filled the apartment with happy music.

"I invited that man from work," said Margie.

"Do you think he'll come?"

"I hope so. I think I might kind of like him," said Margie. "Louise, how do you know Jack is the one? How do you know he's the one you want to be with forever?"

"You just know. He'll make you feel like the most important person in the world. He'll make you feel like nothing else matters except you. And when he touches you, you'll tingle all the way to your toes," said Louise.

"And no other boy has ever made you feel that way?"

"Not really," said Louise. "And I've kissed a lot of boys." She giggled. They both giggled. Then Louise stopped abruptly. "Margie, you know that dream I had last night?"

"Yes"

"I think I'm having it again," she said as she pointed to the doorway at the other end of the bathroom. The blue light was back. Louise didn't scream this time. She just stood there in the kitchen watching. "It wasn't a dream, was it?"

Margie shook her head, "No, it wasn't."

"We're moving," said Louise.

"No, we're not," said Margie. "I like this place. I want to find out what that thing is, and then I want to see what we need to do about it. Maybe it's something good. What if it's a saint or something?"

"You're joking, right?"

Someone knocked at the door. Both girls screamed. Had they lost track of time? Their hair still in curlers, they looked at the clock. It was only seven. Who would come early? Margie went to the door. It was Pearl.

"I thought I'd come early and see if you needed any help," said Pearl. "And I brought some snacks and a little something for the punch," she held out a food tray in one hand and a bottle in the other. "You two better get ready. I'll work on the food."

"Wait!" both girls screamed together. "Don't go in there!"

They were too late because Pearl was already in the kitchen. They caught up with her only to discover the blue light had disappeared. Would it stay gone for the party?

"She's right," said Louise. "We need to get ready. Pearl may not be the only one to come early."

The bathroom was a long room with three entry doors. They would lock two of them for the party to keep the confusion down. Right now, all three doors were open, which made it easy to talk with Pearl while they were getting ready.

"Pearl, have you and Art set a date yet? And, where is he? Isn't he coming?" asked Louise.

"He'll be here later. He dropped me off, but he and a couple of guys are going on a beer run. They won't bring it in the house. They'll just have it in the car. And no, we haven't set a date yet. I want him to finish college first."

"You're so lucky to have a college man," said Margie.

"I know," said Pearl. "Only the best for us. We just have to put in the time. And he only has one year left. We'll probably get married right after that."

There was a knock at the door. Pearl looked at the clock. "It's only a quarter 'til seven," she called out to Louise and Margie. "I'll get it." She went to the door and propped it open. "Come on in. We're still setting it up," she said to Mary.

"I brought some streamers," said Mary, "just to add to the festivity."

Mary and Pearl ran off to the living room to hang the streamers. Louise and Margie emerged from the bedroom looking like the queens of the ball. Margie ran to the bathroom to put their makeup and curlers away and lock two of the doors, especially the one where the blue light had been appearing.

As more people arrive, each one seemed to be bringing something. From Gale, there were party hats. Peter brought noisemakers and something to spike the punch. Jack brought flowers. Of course, those were for Louise. Mr. Flaherty didn't seem to be coming. Margie was disappointed. Then at eight-thirty, he arrived. He brought a camera from the newsroom.

"Does Mr. King know you have that?" asked Margie.

"Yes, of course. I told Mr. King I would be covering the New Year's Eve celebrations." He winked as he said it.

"Mr. Flaherty?" asked Margie. "Can I ask you a question?"

"No, but you can ask Mark a question. Please, call me Mark, won't you?" said Mr. Flaherty.

"Alright," said Margie. "Mark? If the light shows up tonight, will you be able to take a picture of it with this camera?"

"That's why I brought it," said Mark proudly. "Now, is there one place it shows up more than others?"

"It always shows up in that doorway right there," she said, pointing to the door from the living room side.

"Is that door usually closed?"

"No, it's one of three doors to the bathroom, though. So tonight, we're keeping it closed."

"Well, I'll keep an eye on it. Is there a particular time it usually shows up?

"It's already shown up once tonight. Louise saw it this time for real, which means she wants to move," said Margie. "I told her I wanted to find out what it is. I mean, what if it's a saint or something like that, right?"

Mark just stared at her for a minute. "I guess anything is possible," he finally said. "Maybe we'll get lucky, and it will come back during the party."

"If not, maybe you could stay for a while after the party," suggested Margie. "We could camp out in the living room for an hour or two. It could be like a stakeout."

"We could," he said. "Let's see what happens."

Everyone enjoyed the party, and although the other tenants didn't come, no one complained about the noise. Some of the boys had brought bottle rockets to set off at midnight. They had them set up downstairs by the back porch. At ten 'til eleven, they turned on the radio to listen to the countdown from New York. They all yelled and waved and used their noisemakers, but they saved the rockets for midnight their time.

At ten 'til midnight, they found the Dallas station, and at five 'til they moved the party outside to the back yard. At ten seconds 'til they started the countdown along with the radio. The neighbors all came out to count it down with them.

At midnight they launched the bottle rockets, and everyone made as much noise as they could to wake up the New Year. Some couples kissed. The whole party sang Auld Lang Syne, then moved back into the house.

"Let's go get the black-eyed peas," said Louise. "We've been cooking them all afternoon. Let's get the New Year's good fortune flowing."

Everyone had a small helping of black-eyed peas to ensure wealth in nineteen-forty. Most didn't care for the taste, but they all ate their portion.

After that, people started leaving. The boys would carry the party on through New Year's Day with the playing of the Rose Bowl. But for now, the party was winding down.

By twelve-thirty, everyone was gone except Louise and Jack, and Margie and Mark. Louise and Jack excused themselves to the bedroom. Margie and Mark opened the door to the bedroom and settled in to stake out the space for the blue light.

Louise seemed to have forgotten about it. That or she just felt safe with Jack there. Either way, she wasn't concerned about moving right now. Margie was glad to have Mark there. It would have been awkward for Jack to stay if Margie had been alone. She put some pillows from the sofa on

219

the floor to make herself and Mark comfortable. They could see the doorway but weren't blatantly visible themselves.

At one-thirty, Jack and Louise walked out of the bedroom without noticing Margie and Mark. Louise walked Jack to the door and lingered there with him for a few more minutes. Then she turned to go back to the bedroom. Just as she turned Mark flashed a picture of the bathroom door. Louise jumped and screamed simultaneously. Margie ran to Louise to quiet her. The blue light had returned. Margie wanted a picture of that more than anything.

Mark snapped several more shots and then stopped. The blue orb had disappeared, but he had seen it in person. Louise missed it and was startled by the flash.

"What are you doing here? Do you know what time it is? How rude to take my picture like this! What were you thinking? You cannot use those pictures!!!!" Louise was alternating between screaming, yelling and crying.

"It wasn't a picture of you," said Margie trying to calm her down. "We wouldn't do that to you. Just go on to bed. I'll explain it all in the morning."

"Mark, did you see it? Do you think you got it?" Margie asked.

"I don't know if I got it, but I certainly saw it," said Mark. "You can't stay here, Margie. That thing was real, and we don't know what it is. It may not be safe."

"Let's see what develops from the film first, okay?" said Margie knowing she had no plans of leaving. This was an incredible find. She wanted to learn everything she could about it.

"I don't think it's a good idea," said Mark.

"When can you develop the film?" she asked, smiling her biggest smile and batting her pretty blue eyes.

"I'll do it first thing in the morning." He had to work anyway. Besides, he was just as curious as she was to see what was on that film. The editor here at this newspaper might not be interested in something supernatural, but other papers would buy the story, especially if he had a photograph. He would be more than happy to develop the film in the morning. Besides, he owed his editor a New Year's Eve story, and there were pictures from the party on this roll.

"What time will you get there? I can come in early and help," said Margie, not wanting the night to end.

"I'm supposed to be there at eleven, but I thought I could go in at ten and get it done before anyone showed up."

"I'll be there at ten myself then," said Margie.

She walked him to the door and lingered for a few minutes, hoping for a "goodnight" kiss. He didn't want to move too fast with one so young. So, they just stared into each other's eyes for a minute. Then he left.

Margie stood with her back to the door and sighed a long low sigh. She would have been happy for him to stay all night, and wouldn't have cared what people might think. Every time they touched for even a second, her skin tingled from head to toe. She thought he might be the one.

She took a few minutes to notice the light coming from the bathroom. She walked over slowly and as quietly as possible. There in the bathroom, she saw more than just a ball of light. It looked like a little boy, or at least the upper half of a little boy. He was facing away from her, and he was made up of blue light. It was beautiful. She should have been afraid, but she wasn't. She couldn't stop staring. Then it turned to look at her. When it smiled, the teeth were sharp and jagged giving it a sinister look. She screamed, and it disappeared.

She decided maybe they should move after all. What had seemed so beautiful had turned into something menacing. She slept fitfully that night.

New Year's Day she was at the Newspaper office by ten. Mark was inside already, having left the back door open. She went in and found him in the darkroom. The light wasn't on, so she walked in. He was preparing the room for the developing process. He had waited for her to get there before starting the actual procedure. She paused to tell him what had happened after he left.

He was all business as he worked with the chemicals. He handed her some gloves and an apron. He didn't expect her to do anything, but he wanted her protected just in case. He passed the first print page through the chemical pans and hung it on the line to dry. It was only one of the many pictures from the party. Margie recognized her friends. They would be so surprised to have their image in the paper.

The next one was Margie and Louise laughing. There were lots of pictures of the party. They were interesting, but not what Margie and Mark were anxious to see. At long last, they came to the one doorway. It was there! The ball of light was there! Margie jumped for joy and hugged Mark. In the excitement, they kissed one another.

They stopped. *Did that just happen?* thought Margie.

"I'm sorry," said Mark. "I got a little caught up with the moment."

"Don't be sorry," said Margie shyly, rocking from side to side. "I enjoyed it."

Mark finished up the pictures. After they were dry, he chose three to give to the editor. The Editor might select one for the front page if Mark was lucky. He pulled the three that were for his other story and put them in an envelope in his desk.

He walked up to Margie's desk and said, "Can we get together at your place after work? I want to look at these photos more closely."

"That would be great," said Margie.

"I'll drive you home," he said.

Margie couldn't wait for the day to end so she could spend more time with Mark. She still hadn't told him what she had seen. She hadn't told anyone, thinking about it made her realize, maybe, hopefully, that part had been her imagination mixed with a bit of spiked punch.

Mark motioned her to go at four. The Rose Bowl would be starting, and no one would be paying attention to anything else. They left with the packet full of pictures in hand and went straight to Margie's place. Louise was gone, probably listening to the game with Jack and his friends.

Mark pulled out the photographs. He could only find it in the first print. The other two were empty and a little out of focus. But the first one was sharp and clear. It was a circle of light with soft edges and a hint of what was behind it, showing through. He brought out a magnifying glass. "There might actually be a face in it," he said.

"Mark, I need to tell you about what I saw last night after you left."

"Did the light come back?"

"It was more than just a light. It was, well, it seemed like, well,"

"Just spit it out," said Mark anxiously.

"It was the top half of a little boy, only he was made of light. He was looking away from me, then he turned to look at me. He seemed so sweet. Then he smiled showing such sharp teeth, like an animal. It scared me. You may be right about me needing to move. Whatever this is, it isn't nice, and it's no saint. I hardly slept last night for fear it might come back."

"I'll stay here on the sofa tonight," said Mark. "I won't leave you here alone with it."

"I need to talk to the landlord," said Margie. "I really need to move right away." Walking into the bedroom, she found a note on the dresser from Louise.

"I'm sorry, Margie. I won't stay here another day. That thing called my name this morning as I was waking up. It sounded like a mean little boy. It called my name and then laughed. I have most of my things. I'll be back for the rest tomorrow when Jack is off work."

"Wow," said Margie, "I guess that seals the deal. I'm definitely not staying here by myself."

"Whose furniture is this?" asked Mark.

"It's a furnished apartment," said Margie. "Now I have to find another one and fast. Louise can just move back in with her Mom and Dad. I won't do that." she started to cry.

"Let's just take this one step at a time," said Mark. "I'll stay here tonight. I'll need to go get a few things, but it won't take long. You can come with me. Then tomorrow, we'll find you a new place."

"Are there any rooms available where you live?" she asked.

"Not for you. I live in a men's boarding house. You work the classifieds, don't you? Have you seen any ads for a room in a ladies boarding house or an apartment?"

"I can't remember right now," said Margie.

Mark stopped at the office on the way to his place. "Wait here. I'll be right back."

He returned with the paper's classified section. "Now you have a place to start looking."

He drove to his boarding house, stopped the car again, and asked her to wait. It only took a few minutes to go up to his room, get his shaving kit and a change of clothes. Then they were on their way back to Margie's place.

Once inside, they took seats on the sofa. Margie was afraid to look in the direction of the bathroom. She didn't want to see whatever it was ever again.

"Let's look through the paper," suggested Mark.

They read every ad. There was nothing that sounded right. Most of the rents were too high. This apartment really was a good deal, but they both knew why. They talked about the party the night before and how much fun they had both had. Mark reached for Margie's hand. She did not withdraw. He kissed her, and she kissed back. He was definitely the one.

She felt like she was glowing. *Wait*, she thought. *I am glowing. Where is this coming from?*

"Mark, it's here. Look"

Before them stood a little boy made of blue light. He tilted his head and began to smile.

"Stop right there, young man!" ordered Margie. "You are not going to scare me out of my home! You are welcome to stay here, but you will NOT do anything to scare my friends or me! Do you understand?" The little boy lowered his head as if in shame and nodded.

"And don't you ever show your teeth around me again! Do you understand?"

Once again, the little boy nodded.

"Good. As long as we both understand who's in charge, this will work just fine."

He turned and floated away with a sawtooth grin from ear to ear.

The End

Story 9

Henry Was Cold

It was cold outside… which meant that it was also cold inside. She hated that about this house. She was chilled to the bone. There was no central heat, and these little gas space heaters just didn't do the job.

Taking a shower was a nightmare! The hot water felt wonderful, but as soon as you turned it off, you were freezing. So she would use the dryer on her hair, and that would warm her up while she was doing it. There was just no getting around the cold.

Sometimes she envied the cat who could sleep on top of the heater and seemed to stay pretty cozy. The cat's name was Bitsy. She was typically lazy, but Jennifer loved having her around. She made the house a little less scary and a lot cozier.

Jennifer had started wearing granny pajamas in the evening because the house was so cold. She used an electric blanket on the bed which helped. But before bed, she needed the heavy PJs to keep her warm. She wasn't going out tonight, so she just went straight for the PJs after her shower.

As she settled into the comfy recliner and picked up a book to read, there was a knock at the door. "Dang!" she said. "If I'd known someone was coming over, I'd have put real clothes on. Who's there?" she called.

"Annie," came a small voice from the other side of the door.

Jennifer climbed out of the recliner and unlocked the door. "Come on in. What are you doing out in this cold?"

"Dang," said Annie. "It's colder in here than it is outside. Why don't you turn on a heater?"

"I have every heater on," said Jennifer. "It just won't warm up."

"You need to talk to your landlord. There is something wrong with the insulation or something."

"Yeah, maybe I will."

"Why don't you go get dressed. We'll go to a movie? There's one I want to see. I know you'll like it. It has vampires in it."

"I don't have any money for it this week, Annie. I don't get paid for another week." She explained

"I just got paid. I can pay for both. Next time will be your treat, but hurry up. I don't want to miss the beginning," said Annie.

Jennifer ran to her bedroom and found something to wear. They took Annie's car, and sure enough, it was warmer outside than it had been in her duplex.

The theater felt great, and the movie was watchable. They were almost the only ones in the room. There was a couple behind them that didn't sound like they were there to watch the movie, and a creepy old man was sitting near the exit. Still, Jennifer enjoyed it and thanked Annie for getting her out of the house.

"No problem," said Annie. "I know how it is when you're between paychecks. You'll rescue me when you have some money."

"Yes, I will," said Jennifer.

They walked out into the cold, and all the wonderful warmth from the theater vanished from her bones. Jennifer had accepted that she was just cold natured. Annie turned the heat up in the car and drove back to Jennifer's place. They walked in and were both surprised to find that the house felt warm and cozy. It was as if someone had come in while they were gone and repaired the problem.

Annie had to be at work early in the morning, so she said Good Night and left. Jennifer changed back into her PJs and curled back up with her book. Within fifteen minutes, the temperature started dropping. Nothing had changed, but it was getting colder again. She put her book aside and went to bed to warm up under the electric blanket.

The next day Annie called. She had thought about it and thought that maybe there was a vampire near Jennifer's place. Vampires could suck the heat right out of a place. "I don't think it's a vampire," said Jennifer. "You're just being influenced by the movie we saw last night. There are no such things as vampires."

"Well, it wouldn't hurt to get some garlic and put around the house," said Annie. "I'm going to call my friend Scott. He knows all about vampires. I'll tell him what's going on and find out what we need to do."

"I really don't think it's a vampire," said Jennifer. I just have a very drafty house."

"I'm going to call him anyway." Said Annie.

"Suit yourself," said Jennifer.

An hour later, Annie called again. "Can I bring Scott over to your place tonight after work?" she asked. "He doesn't think it's a vampire, but he has another idea."

"Sure, but eat before you come over. I don't have anything to fix for a meal."

"No problem," said Annie. "We'll bring something for you, too. Is it cold in there today?"

"Yes, the temperature dropped about half an hour after you left last night. Maybe I just need to get you to come over more often," she chuckled as she said it.

Scott and Annie showed up with burgers and fries. Jennifer had never met Scott. She could see why Annie was so anxious to get him involved. He had a rugged, handsome quality, and wasn't afraid to talk. This could be an interesting evening.

"Is it usually colder in one place in the house more than others?" Scott asked.

"I'm not sure," said Jennifer. "I just get chilled to the bone and can't find a warm place except standing over the gas heater."

"I'm going to do some tests," said Scott. "I'm going to take some temperature measurements. I'm also going to set up a couple of pieces of equipment to measure things like EM surges, and I'm going to look for possible drafts."

Scott was very serious about this, and Annie was trying hard to be just as serious and be his assistant. Yes, Annie had a crush and Jennifer totally understood. But she doubted that any of this was going to solve her heat problem. She went along to help Annie, and there were, after all, free burgers.

"I'm going to make some hot cocoa," said Jennifer. "Would either of you like a cup?" Annie waited for Scott to answer. He declined, so she declined too.

Jennifer left them in the living room and made her hot cocoa. It always warmed her up for a few minutes. And it was delicious. Even if it was just water and bagged cocoa.

Annie wasn't socializing with Jennifer tonight. She was trying to impress Scott with her investigating skills. So Jennifer curled up again in her recliner, opened her book, and began to read.

"Hello," said Scott. "what do we have here?"

"I'm sorry," said Jennifer. "You didn't seem to need my help, so I was just going to read. Did I mess something up?"

"Not at all," said Scott. "My equipment reacted to you in a very interesting way. The cold area seems to be following you. In fact, I could feel the cold coming from you as you walked by. That's why I measured."

"What does that mean?" said Annie and Jennifer together.

"It means that there may be a spirit here who is trying to get energy. I notice you don't have a radio on or a tv. Is that how it usually is?"

"A spirit?" said Jennifer. "You mean like a ghost?"

"I prefer the word spirit, but yes, people call them ghosts. The question is, do you ordinarily sit here without a lot of electrical things turned on?"

"I like to read at night. I don't like the distractions of the TV or the radio. I have my electric blanket on the bed, and a few clocks and the refrigerator. Everything else is gas."

"It seems that there is a spirit here, and YOU are the only energy source most of the time. Will you let me do an experiment?"

"What kind of experiment? I really don't believe in ghosts or any of this hoodoo stuff."

"I want to set up an EM pump to "feed" the spirit and see if that will keep them from feeding on you."

"Them?" said Jennifer. "Like more than one?"

"Maybe. Let's just try this and see what happens with the temperatures around you. Okay?"

"Okay," said Jennifer hesitantly.

Annie was excited and terrified at the same time. She was really leaning toward the vampire theory, which wasn't as scary because she didn't really believe in them, but ghosts? Ghosts were real, and she was afraid of them.

Scott set up the EM pump and turned it on. It made a buzzing sound, but it wasn't bad. Scott monitored the temperatures around Jennifer and the energy around the EM pump. After a few minutes, Jennifer began to notice a slight rise in temperature. Just then, the lights flickered.

"Is that thing overloading my breakers," she asked.

"It shouldn't be. If I'm right, that might have been the spirit saying thank you."

"Well, the spirit needs to move on or at least move someplace else," said Jennifer. "What am I supposed to do? Buy one of your gadgets and leave it on all winter?"

"Or you could turn on the TV. Just keep it on mute so it won't distract you. That might produce enough energy for it to draw and be satisfied."

"I don't want a satisfied ghost…"

"Spirit"

"I don't want a satisfied spirit. I want a GONE spirit. Can you get rid of it?"

"No, but I might know someone who can. Let me make some phone calls tomorrow. In the meantime, I will let you borrow the pump."

"Well… It does feel warmer in here," she said.

"I don't think it means any harm," said Scott. "It just needs the energy to move about. It doesn't really think about it making you cold."

"So, you think it's safe, and you're just going to leave me here with a ghost?"

"I could stay for a while and do an EVP session and see if we can learn what they want. Annie, would you mind staying?"

"I'd love to," said the extremely smitten Annie. "You could teach me how to do it."

Scott pulled out his recorder and turned it on. He started asking questions about who was there with them, and could they talk into the recorder or do something to let them know they were there.

The wind picked up outside, and they could all feel one of those drafts they had found earlier. Scott thought it was a sign from the spirit, but Jennifer preferred to think it was just the wind.

After about half an hour, Scott turned off the recorder and began to play it back. He had two headsets plugged in so that he and Annie could listen closely to the audio. At about seven minutes in, they both heard a strange voice say, "my house, too." They replayed it several times and let Jennifer listen to it. She heard the same thing they did.

They continued to listen. At thirteen minutes, they heard, "Protect you." Once again, they played it several times to be sure of what they were hearing. It was as if the spirit had been sitting with them, they could hear it that clearly.

At twenty-two minutes, the three had been talking about what would happen if it was a mean spirit. Just then, they heard, "no problem." Was the spirit telling them that it was not mean?

At twenty-six minutes in, Jennifer was saying that she might need to move if it was something mean. The spirit said, "Don't go."

"Do you still want me to call around for a spirit sweeper?" Scott asked.

"This is all too much to take in," said Jennifer. "I don't know what to do. It sounds like it means no harm and might even be friendly. Let me sleep on it."

Scott and Annie packed up everything but the EM pump and left Jennifer alone with her newfound spirit friend. Except she still wasn't feeling the friendly part yet.

When Annie called Jennifer the next day, there was no answer. She tried her at work and was told that Jennifer had not made it in today. She hadn't called either. This was not like Jennifer and Annie was worried. She told Scott, and they agreed to go over at lunchtime.

They knocked on the door for at least five minutes before Annie pulled out her spare key. They walked into the house and felt the warmth of it hit them in the face immediately. Annie was in tears before she ever opened the door. Something was obviously wrong.

She burst into the room only to find Jennifer sitting on the floor with a deck of cards. She acted like she didn't see or hear Annie and Scott. She was talking to no one. She seemed to be playing cards with someone. She would ask if they wanted a card and wait a few seconds and then act as if someone had answered. But there was no one there.

Annie dropped to the floor and grabbed Jennifer by the shoulders. "Jennifer, talk to me. What are you doing?"

"Oh, I didn't see you come in," said Jennifer in a distant voice. "I'm playing cards with Henry. He has let me win a few hands, I think."

"Jennifer, there is no one here, except you and me and Scott."

"Oh. Hello, Scott. I didn't see you there. You met Henry last night, and he was most grateful for all the energy. Says it's amazing. He feels like a new man."

Scott walked over and turned off the EM pump.

"You probably shouldn't have done that," said Jennifer. "I think you've made him angry." Apparently, when Henry is angry, he throws things because a lamp came flying through the room and just missed Scott's ear.

"This won't do," said Scott. "Henry, you can't possess this girl. She has a life and friends and a job. You need to let her go. If you will leave her alone, I will get you another energy source."

Jennifer seemed to snap out of it. "What's going on?" she asked. What are you doing here? What time is it?" Jennifer was back.

Scott turned on the TV. He had promised Henry an alternate energy source. The EM pump was apparently not safe to leave on all the time. Annie took Jennifer to the bedroom to get a change of clothes and led her out of the house.

Jennifer was confused. Was it afternoon? She should be at work. What had she been doing sitting on the living room floor? And it had been so warm.

Annie took Jennifer to work. She explained that Jennifer had been a little out of it this morning, but hopefully, she was back to normal now. She asked them to call her if anything out of the ordinary happened.

Scott called a couple of "experts" to see what they thought of the situation. Everyone agreed that Scott had flooded the rooms with too much energy for too long and had given the spirit a good amount of control over the space. Jennifer had no idea what was going on, so it was easy to pull her into the illusion.

It was decided that Scott should monitor the house for a few days and see that it calmed down and that the spirit did not remain angry. If, in three days, things were not back to "normal," they would bring in a spirit sweeper to cleanse the house.

Of course, they should have consulted with Jennifer, who was getting back to normal herself. Jennifer wanted no part of them. They had already done enough damage as far as she was concerned. They would not be allowed to monitor anything. They did not need to come back to her house. Scott suggested that she at least leave the TV on to appease the spirit and keep the temperatures up a bit.

She agreed to do that. She went home that night, and as she walked in the door, she was greeted by just a faint chill in the air. *Ah*, she thought. *Back to normal.* The TV was still on from earlier in the day. She debated whether to leave it on or not. A voice from somewhere behind her said, "leave it on."

The End

Story 10

The Storm

After several months without rain, it was exciting to have some on the way. The garden needed water, but she decided to hold off and let Mother Nature take care of it. She had forgotten how cruel Mother Nature could be with her rains.

The ground had gone so long without water that it couldn't absorb the rain fast enough. The yard turned into a small lake with a stream running to it. The street was underwater within an hour. This would be a flood, for sure, and some would have to leave their homes for higher ground. It happened at least once a year. The street flooding was bad enough, but when it came up into your house and ruined your floors and furniture, it was heartbreaking. There would be a neighbor or two that would face that by nightfall.

Sharon knew that her house was safe from it. The backyard might flood, but it would never reach her home. The first time it happened, she was scared. It looked like it was coming in, but then it stopped. That was the highest she had ever seen it, and she had been here for over ten years.

Without warning, the rain stopped. The sky didn't clear, but the rain stopped. Maybe it wouldn't flood this time. She breathed a sigh of relief not for herself, but for the neighbors. The ground definitely needed the water, and it needed this break in the rain to soften up and be able to accept more. The forecast was for rain all week. But if it came in bursts like this, it would be okay.

She went back to her painting. She had been painting the trim inside her house when the storm started. She loved thunderstorms, so she had stopped to watch. She had even sat out on the porch for a bit. This was her favorite kind of weather. She loved sitting on the porch in a thunderstorm. She had a rocking chair and, on this occasion, the cat had joined her, which only enhanced the experience.

But now, it was time to get back to painting. Painting baseboards always fell to her. Being short and not minding scooting around on the floor and having a steady hand enough so to do it without taping, made her the obvious choice. She had a technique down. She would wipe down the baseboards on one full side of the room with a wet cloth to clean them. The board would be dry by the time she finished wiping it, then she would scoot back over to the beginning and start painting.

After ten years, they had decided to paint the whole house inside and out, and the trim was the last step. Someone knocked on the door and she groaned to have to get up and go answer it, but she was the only one there, so… She made it to the door to find no one was there. Maybe she had imagined it. It was still drizzling rain, and there was also still some thunder to be heard. It had been a very soft knock. They had had that happen before with the doorbell, too. It would sound off after ten at night, and they would go to the door, and there would be no one in sight. It was, at the very least, annoying.

Sharon stepped back out on the porch and sat in the rocker. *No sense wasting a forced break*, she thought. The cat meandered over and rubbed her legs a few times weaving in and out, her tail just missing the rocker arm. Finally, she jumped up in Sharon's lap and started purring loud enough to be heard from the walkway. Whatever the sound was that interrupted her, Sharon was grateful for it.

These moments were the reason for owning a home.

The rain picked up again, and she realized there was quite a bit of chill to the air. She was reluctant to leave the comfort of the porch. She knew if she went back inside, she would just go back to painting, and this was so much nicer. Besides, the cat was so cozy. Sharon didn't want to disturb her. The rain began falling hard. It started blowing in on the porch, and even the cat jumped down and retreated to cover. Sharon went back inside.

She picked up the trim brush and went back to work. The house had such a nice clean feel to it with all the new paint. She had thought about getting Bill to replace the tile in the bathroom shower, too. He would do it if she asked. And it **was** ten years old, or more... Maybe she would mention it tonight. She finished up the last wall in the dining room and decided to call it a day on painting.

There was already a meal in the crockpot for tonight, and she wanted to spend the rest of the day enjoying the weather, not scooting through the house painting. The house was eerily dark from the clouds and storms. She had had the light on in the room where she was working, but the rest of the house didn't usually need the lights on during the day. Dark as it was, she saw a shadow move at the other end of the hall. *Could someone be in the house?* She thought. *No, no, they couldn't have gotten in without her seeing.*

She walked towards the back of the house. As she entered the kitchen, she turned on the lights. No one was there. She went through the house, turning on the lights. That shadow had spooked her, and she wasn't too proud to turn on every light in the house. She had always been afraid of the dark. As far back as her memory reached, the darkness had terrified her without knowing why. She knew logically that there was nothing in the night that wasn't there in the light. But somehow, that didn't comfort her. She would take the light please.

If anything shadowy showed up with all this light, she would be leaving. But, it's funny how the scary shadows don't show up when there's plenty of light. It's only when there's a storm or after dusk that the shadows like to play with us. That's why Sharon was afraid of the dark.

Bill would be home soon. She had enjoyed her day "off." Time to get ready for the nightly routine. Bill would arrive around six in time for dinner, where they would discuss their days. Bill would watch the recorded news. They would see if there were any shows to watch. If not, they would surf the internet. By eleven or midnight, they would be in bed. Unless one of them had a meeting or they had guests over. Then the whole routine was out the window. One week, they had had plans every night, and by Saturday, they were exhausted. They had missed their routine.

This night was not going to be entirely routine. After dinner, Bill had a meeting to attend in Old Town. Sharon would not be going with him, so she would be home alone for the evening thunderstorms. She found a completely harmless movie to put on after Bill left. Just something to keep her company, as it were.

Bill made it home in between storms, and they had dinner. He was running late, so they didn't have much time to talk. She decided it wasn't the right time to talk about redoing the tiles. He had remarked about all the lights being on, and she had blown it off to her moving from room to room to paint. She didn't want to admit she had been spooked. He wouldn't make fun of her, but she knew he would think she was silly.

Bill left, and Sharon poured a glass of wine before sitting down to her movie. She had chosen a long one so that it would last until Bill returned. As the opening credits rolled, a bolt of lightning hit so close to the house that she jumped out of her seat. Almost instantly, the power went off. Sharon felt her heart creep up to her throat. It was darker than usual because of the storm. She sat there like a stone. She was afraid to move.

Where is the flashlight? She thought. *Or a candle, that would work. Why was she sitting in the darkest room in the house without so much as a candle?*

The lights flickered for a moment. Her heart lightened. Then the lights went out again. Sirens were going off, and she could hear the wind through the windows making a whistling sound. This was not what she had planned for the evening at all. She tugged the blanket off the back of the sofa and wrapped it around her like some protective shield. As she rose from the couch, she pulled the blanket over her head and crouched low. Had the lights been on, she would have looked and felt ridiculous, but as it was, she felt much safer with her shield and her crouching motion.

She crept cautiously into the kitchen. Maybe there would be something in the junk drawer to give her some light. She found the drawer and felt her way around it. Aha! There was a lighter. Now, where had she put that scented candle she bought for last Christmas and forgot to use? She had just seen it yesterday when moving things to paint. It was on the baker's rack. She crept over to the baker's rack. She knocked the jar of yeast to the floor as she felt around for the candle.

Please be here. Please be here. She thought. She found it behind a basket of nuts. (also, from last Christmas). She lit the candle, and for a second, thought she saw someone staring at her from a few feet away, but there was no one there. Her heart was racing now. But at least she had some light.

Now she could use this light to look for a flashlight. There should be one in the cupboard, but they were always using it and forgetting to return it. She decided to check the cabinet anyway. She turned, and this time, she screamed as she saw a face a few feet away from her. Then she realized it was her own reflection in the back-door window. She needed something stronger than wine. But first, a flashlight.

It wasn't in the cupboard. She went to the back door and checked the catch-all shelf. There it was. The batteries were weak, but it was light, and that was good. Now to find more candles. She went into the living room armed with both candles and flashlight, but she still had her shield over her head. She felt a little better, but not enough to drop her protective armor.

There were three candles in the living room that they never actually lit. She lit those and was surprised at how much light they gave. The room was almost as bright as it was when they would watch TV in the dark. There were lots of flickering shadows, but there was also light. She might survive this night.

Searching the bedroom, there were five large candles to be found. They hadn't been lit in a long time, but once lit, it was pretty bright. Sitting on the bed for a minute, she thought about what to do next. *Were there any more candles? Or flashlights?* She thought. Maybe in the dining room. She made her way to the dining room and saw Bill come in the front door. She ran to greet him and get a much-needed hug. Reaching for him, he was gone. She checked the front door, and it was locked. The lack of light was playing tricks on her. She started to panic. The rain came down harder now. She could hear it beating on the windows and the porch. She didn't know what to do.

Wait! The phone! Where was the phone? She thought. She realized it had been dying earlier, and she had forgotten to plug it in to charge. She couldn't call Bill. She couldn't use it to go on the internet.

There was a knock at the door, and Sharon screamed again. She looked through the window, and there was actually someone standing there. Opening the door revealed her neighbor. His power was out as well. He had brought over a candle in case she needed one. He knew she was home alone and didn't want her to be alone in the dark. He had called the power company, and they said that it might be hours before power was restored.

Sharon thanked him for the candle, but she had found several.

"Are you okay?" asked Dan, the neighbor.

"Yes, of course," she replied.

"It's just, well, I thought I heard screaming."

"I get a little jumpy when the power goes out in a storm," said Sharon with as much confidence as she could muster. "I'm fine, really. I'll be even better when the power comes back on."

"Would you like to come over to my house and wait for Bill there? That way, you wouldn't have to be alone."

Sharon and Bill had never gotten to know their new neighbor. They knew each other's names, but that was about as far as they had gotten. Dan kept to himself. He was renting the house since a few months ago, and he didn't do any of the lawncare himself. He parked in the garage, and it was hard to tell when he was home. Sharon felt as uneasy about being alone with him in the dark in his house as she did about being alone in the dark in her own house. In fact, she decided she'd rather be alone in her own home.

"No," she said. "Bill will be home soon, and I will be okay until then. Thank you for offering, though. That's very thoughtful."

"Are you sure?" he pressed her. "I feel bad for you being over here and being jumpy as you call it. Maybe I should stay here with you," he suggested.

"I'm fine, really," she insisted. She wanted to get off the porch and back inside. "Thank you very much for offering." She slipped back into the house and locked the door.

She honestly felt terrified inside the house and outside the house. She felt small and wished Bill would come home. The lights flickered on. Sharon let out a deep sigh. Much better. Then the lights flickered off again. This was not funny. She walked towards the bedroom where the most candles were lit. They were all still burning. She sat on the edge of the bed and felt as alone as she had ever felt.

It was a shame they didn't know Dan any better, but they didn't, and she was not going to let the first time she walked in his house be in the middle of a power outage. She looked out the bedroom window and saw some light filtering through the curtains of one of his windows. She didn't know which room that was as she had never been inside his house. Whatever room it was, he must be in there because she saw his shadow move across the room. She felt like she was spying and turned away from the window.

As she turned, she saw a shadowy figure in her own room. *Just shadows from the candles playing tricks,* she told herself. *Calm down. Nothing to worry about.* She wasn't very convincing, and she could feel her panic rising. Should she have let the neighbor in? Was she too cautious? It felt like someone was watching her. She pulled her blanket up around her head. Where was the flashlight? Ah, she found it, turned it on, and started for the kitchen.

Sharon found more candles and set them up in the kitchen. *Do something routine,* she told herself. But there was nothing routine that could be done in the dark with no electricity. *Read a book,* she thought. *Maybe a romance novel.* She found one and sat at the kitchen table to read it. It helped her relax. She looked up from the book to see a man standing by the stove. Without a sound, this time, she just stared. He didn't disappear and just stood there looking at her. She realized that she could see through him. He was a specter. Was he a ghost?

She said, "hello."

He didn't move. Sharon was afraid to get up or approach him. She was scared to move at all. After an eternal ten or fifteen seconds, he raised his arm and pointed to the bedroom. At least it looked like he was pointing at the bedroom. He could have been showing her a house three blocks away for all she knew. She overcame her fear and walked to the bedroom. The specter didn't move, nor did it disappear. It stood there, pointing.

"I don't know what you want," said Sharon. "Is there something you want me to see?"

The specter disappeared. That startled Sharon as much as the appearance had. She had just been getting used to it being there. Now it appeared by the window in the bedroom. It was pointing at the floor now. Sharon didn't want to get any closer to it, but she couldn't see what it was looking at. Walking to the foot of the bed gave her a better vantage point, but there was nothing there. He was pointing at nothing.

"There's nothing there," she shouted. "What do you want? What do you want me to see? What do you want me to do? This is not funny."

The apparition disappeared. Sharon walked over to the spot it had been pointing to. She shone the flashlight on it and saw a board that looked a bit crooked. It wasn't really noticeable unless you were looking closely. She knelt down to touch it, and it was loose. She tugged at it and felt it give. She tugged a little harder and pulled out a small section of the floor. There was a secret compartment.

Shining the flashlight into the opening, Sharon saw a vintage cigar box. She withdrew the box and opened it. Looking closer, there were a few pieces of paper, a key, and a hunting knife. Closing the box and taking it to the kitchen table, it seemed the key was old, as were the papers. Opening one of the documents, it was, apparently, a receipt from a hardware store. The next piece was a receipt for a safe deposit box with a local bank. *Maybe that's what the key is for*, she thought. Putting the key and the receipt together, she stood to walk back to the bedroom, and the specter appeared again, pointing to the papers on the table. Sharon took the hint and sat back down, continuing to look through the old documents. The next one was a flyer about a church social. Everything was dated from the nineteen-sixties.

As she continued to examine the papers, she found one that compelled her to stop. There was a picture of the specter. It was in a newspaper clipping. Mr. William (Bill) Horowitz would be entering the mayoral race. "Wow," whispered Sharon. "A mayor once lived in this house."

Sharon had stopped thinking of her visitor as a ghost. She was thinking of him as an average man now. She was exceedingly anxious for her husband to get home now. She wanted to share this with him. Would they be able to retrieve whatever was in the safe deposit box? Would there be anything in it? Sharon's anxiety was giving way to excitement. The lights flickered back on, and that light was almost blinding compared to the candlelight she had been using.

Now that there was some light to see by, Sharon looked more closely at the key. It did seem to be a safety deposit box. The name on all the receipts was William Horowitz. As she sat there pondering, he appeared again at the doorway to the bedroom. Once again, he was pointing to the bedroom window. She was not afraid anymore. Walking into the bedroom, she went straight to the hidey-hole she had found. There in the corner was a small pocket watch. She opened it, gasped, and dropped it. Once again, Sharon was afraid.

She scooped up the watch and returned to the kitchen. This made no sense. The picture in the pocket watch was Sharon. She stared at it. *How could this be?* she thought. She wasn't even born yet in the sixties. Her mother wasn't even born until the late fifty's. This was a picture of Sharon in her thirties'. William (Bill) Horowitz showed himself one more time that evening. This time he just stood there briefly with his arms folded and a smile on his face. Sharon didn't get it. Why was he so pleased? All he had done was scare the daylights out of her and hand her a considerable mystery to solve.

With the power back on, she hooked up her phone to charge and then sat down to the internet. Where to start, where to start... She typed in his name. She expected to find something about how he didn't win the mayoral race since there were no clippings about winning in the cigar box. What she found instead was a headline about a man being shot dead in his own home, which was now **her** own home. The revelation had caught her off guard. Was this why he had appeared? Did the thunderstorm remind him of the night he died? And why had he died? What had his murderer wanted? Were they looking for the safe deposit key? And why did he have her picture in his pocket watch?

She combed through the internet, looking for more information. Her husband came in as she was giving up on the mystery. She brought him up to speed on her evening and the mysterious box. She left out any mention of the specter communicating with her.

"Maybe we can go to the bank and see what the key went to?" she asked hopefully.

"Maybe," said her husband. "I wonder who the woman in the photo is since we know she isn't you. Could it be that a relative was involved with him back then?"

His question hung in the air for an uncomfortable length of time. Sharon was afraid to look at that question.

"Well, the bank is a good place to start," he said. "We'll go tomorrow at lunchtime."

"Thank you," she said. "I'll keep looking for information online, too."

Sharon found a small blurb in the society section of a local newspaper; LOCAL MURDER VICTIM MAY HAVE HAD SECRET LOVER. William (Bill) Horowitz, a local banker and mayoral candidate, may have been involved with someone's wife. Rumors run rampant as police fail to find significant clues to the murder that took place in his home two weeks ago. Some say that he had frequently received a female visitor. Others say that she would always wear a scarf that conveniently hid her face. The police had no comment on the reports.

Is that why he was killed? Was there a jealous husband involved? The article was dated August thirty-one, nineteen-sixty-eight. That seemed familiar. But why? It was way before she was born. She seemed to remember it as some kind of an anniversary for someone in the family. She would ask her mother the next time they talked.

Sharon was just happy to have her husband home. She had been stressed for far too long this evening. "Bill, how much do you know about Dan?"

"Dan who?" said Bill.

"There's my answer," said Sharon, "Dan, our next-door neighbor."

"Oh," said Bill. "We've talked at the mailbox a few times, and I've seen him at a Chamber meeting. Other than that, we haven't had any interaction. He seems nice enough."

"He came over while the electricity was off to offer me a candle and to see if I was okay."

"That seems pretty nice of him."

"I know, but I was so scared by the storm and the dark that when he knocked, it scared me even more. I wasn't very gracious," she said.

"I'll go over to thank him tomorrow and let him know you didn't mean to be. Should we invite him over for dinner one night?" said Bill.

"If you like," said Sharon, still feeling a little creepy about Dan. He was probably a perfectly nice man. She had just been jumpy and upset.

"Things will look better in the morning," said Bill. "Let's turn in and get some rest."

The next morning was bright and cheery. It was as if the thunderstorm had never happened. Sharon reminded Bill that he had promised to go to the bank with her at lunch.

"I won't forget, dear," he kissed her as he picked up his briefcase. "Do you want to meet me there?"

"Yes," she said. "I should be able to get there from work by five past twelve."

"I'll see you then," he hugged her and left for work.

She arrived at the bank at twelve-o-five, where Bill was chatting with the branch manager, John. They knew each other through the Chamber of Commerce. He had explained the situation to John, so Sharon pulled the receipt and key from her bag.

"Here's the thing," said John, "this is an old receipt. If the payments haven't been kept up, then we would not have kept the box. At least not on purpose. We would have contacted the owner, and failing that, the bank would have drilled the keyholes, removed the box, and sent its contents to storage."

"Can you check anyway?" asked Sharon. "The owner was murdered. Maybe this box was overlooked."

John was not a man to waste time with something like this, but Bill was a friend, so he agreed.

"You have the key?" he asked.

Sharon handed him the key. There was a number on the key that matched a number on the receipt. John motioned them to follow him. They walked into the safe deposit box room and went to the box listed on the key.

"It takes two keys to open the box," he said. He put Sharon's key in one keyhole and the banker's key in the other keyhole. He gave them both a turn to no avail. The box was still locked.

"I have enough information here to retrieve the contents from storage," he told Sharon, who was obviously disappointed. "It may take a few days, and there may be nothing there, but we can at least check."

"That would be wonderful, John," said Bill with genuine gratitude in his voice. "We'll leave it with you." He turned to Sharon, "Let's go have some lunch, Sweetie. John will do what he can."

Sharon spent the rest of the day wondering and worrying about what, if anything, John would find. She had trouble concentrating on work. If there was anything valuable in the box, surely someone would have removed it by now. But she would be happy to see some documents or letters or anything personal.

She called her mother to chat. After a few minutes of pleasantries, Sharon asked, "Mom, there is a date that keeps coming to my mind, and it seems like it's an anniversary."

"What date is that, dear?"

"August thirty-one, nineteen-sixty-eight."

There was a long silence on the phone. "Mom? Are you there?"

"Yes, dear. It's just... what made you think of that date?"

"It came up in an old news clipping I found when doing some research. What is it? What happened on that date?"

"My mother, your grandmother, died on that date. The police said it was suicide. Of course, that was nonsense. Why would she have done that? She loved me very much and would not have done that to me."

"Wow. I wasn't expecting that!" said Sharon. "Mom, what was Grandma's full name?"

"Sharon Dorothy Hawkins. You were named for her."

"Thanks, Mom. I guess I should get back to work. Are you okay?"

"Yes, it's a little disconcerting to think about it again, but I'm fine. I'll talk to you later."

"Okay. Bye, Mom. Love ya',"

Sharon sat back in her chair and pondered what she had learned. What if that was a picture of her grandmother in that pocket watch? Was her Grandmother the woman that Mr. Horrowitz had been seeing? But her Grandmother was married to her Grandfather. This didn't look good at all. "Curse the ghost that led me to that cigar box in the floor," she whispered to herself. Her pen flew off her desk. "That can't be a coincidence," she thought out loud. She frowned and looked at the clock. Close enough. She scooped up her bag and headed for the door.

This ghost seemed to be following her now. She really didn't want anyone in the office to see her talking to a spirit. She sat down in her car and said, "Don't ever do that to me again! If you're going to try to scare me, then I'm not going to keep looking into your murder. Scaring me is just not acceptable. If you understand, move this piece of paper to the floor." The note floated gently to the floor of the car. "Thank you," she said. "It's scary enough that you are here. I want to help you. I really do, but no more scaring me."

Sharon went home and started dinner. Bill came in and had good news from John. There was a box in storage, and he would have it at the bank Thursday by noon. Sharon could barely contain her excitement. She just knew there would be something in the box that would help this spirit move on and had to remind herself that that was the day after tomorrow, and it would be best to just forget about it until then. She thanked Bill again and again for talking to John.

The next day and a half dragged on for an eternity. Finally, she got the call from Bill, "John has the box in hand. Do you want to meet me there?"

"I'll be there in ten minutes," she said.

John had a frown on his face when they approached him. "Since this belonged to a murder victim, I have to show it to the police," he said.

Sharon was crushed.

"But… I don't see any harm in letting you look through it first. You **do** have the key, after all," he said with a wink.

Sharon burst into tears. "Thank you," she said. John led them back into the safe deposit room and left them alone with the box as if it had been secured in the vault. Sharon hesitated to open it. She finally lifted the lid gently and slowly.

On top of a lot of papers and envelopes was a stunning deep blue jeweled bracelet. The receipt underneath was dated August thirty-one, Nineteen-sixty-eight. Sharon held the bracelet in her hand and heard someone whisper in her ear, "Try it on." She complied immediately, then had no desire to take it off. The blue stones were beautiful, and the bracelet fit like it was made for her wrist. She looked at Bill longingly. He nodded approval. She slipped it off her wrist and put it in her pocket. Neither of them could see the harm in it. She hadn't told Bill about the spirit.

They removed the papers and split the pile in half. The top envelope contained a will. Bill opened it, and they looked together. The will named Sharon's mother (by her maiden name) as his sole heir. There followed a list of stocks and properties. Sharon's mouth dropped open. Why would this man have left everything to her mother?

He opened the next envelope to find a certificate of stock ownership in General Electric. It was for one hundred shares. Bill wondered how many times this stock had split and multiplied since Nineteen-sixty-eight. This one envelope contained a small fortune. And there were at least ten more.

Bill asked John to join them so they could show him the papers and especially the Will. John called in an assistant to arrange for a new safe deposit box.

"These need to be kept secure until the police can look at them, but they will not be removing these papers from the bank. Bill, I'll call you when the police have finished with this. I'll have our lawyer look at the will and get some opinions. Do you have a lawyer you want me to call?" said John.

"Yes, I'll call Jack Barlow and have him give you a call," said Bill.

"Julie, the key goes to...." Bill pointed to Sharon. "Sharon," said John to Julie.

Julie gave the key to Sharon, and they returned the papers to the box.

"The police should be here in a few minutes and the bank's lawyer as well. Can you stay with us, Sharon? We'll need you here to lock everything back up when they have finished. They will be taking pictures of each slip of paper for evidence. Then it will all go back in the safe deposit box as if it had been there all along," he said with a wink.

"I'll be happy to," she replied.

It took all afternoon, but Sharon was happy to stay. She had a new bracelet in her pocket and a lot of questions for her mother. And a lot of questions no one in this room could answer. She surfed the net on her phone while the police did their work.

Sharon found a picture of Mr. Horrowitz and just sat there staring at it. There was something familiar about him. The longer she stared, the more she came to realize...this could easily be her mother's father! Why hadn't she seen it before? She wondered if her mother knew. Curiosity won out, and Sharon called her, "Mom?"

"Yes, dear."

"Have you ever heard of a man named William (Bill) Horrowitz?" asked Sharon.

"He was a friend of my parents, dear. He died a couple of weeks before my mother died. If I recall, he was murdered. What are you researching? Why are you dredging up all this unpleasantness? Please, leave it alone. I don't want to think about those times. It was challenging. My mother and father had some terrible fights around that time. And then my mother died. I don't want to talk about it."

"I'm sorry, Mom," said Sharon. It had all begun to make sense now. Having pulled the bracelet out of her pocket and fondled it, it was apparent that the stones were blue star sapphires, her grandmother's birthstone. "Mom?" she asked,

"Did Grandma ever have a blue sapphire bracelet?"

"Funny you should ask. I saw her wearing one about a month before she died, but then I never saw it again. It was beautiful. I couldn't take my eyes off it. When I asked about it, she told me it had to be our secret, but someday maybe it would be mine. But I never saw it again. That's when she and Daddy started fighting all the time. I had forgotten about that."

Well, her mother obviously didn't know, but there was no doubt in Sharon's mind that the specter was her real grandfather. The bracelet slid back into her pocket as if by magic. Her grandfather was watching out for his granddaughter.

The police finished up, and the bank had made copies of the Will for the attorney while Sharon had been solving the mystery of William (Bill) Horrowitz. She returned the box to its wall slot and locked the door. John escorted her out.

She left the bank with a beautiful bracelet that apparently was meant to be with her mother. She felt it in her pocket and thought about taking a little trip this weekend to visit her.

Bill was in the kitchen, creating a couple of chicken chef salads when she arrived home. She could smell something baking, too. It might be useful to let him beat her home more often. She smiled to herself.

"Sharon, your mother is going to be a very wealthy woman if that Will stands up. I did some checking, and those GE stocks are worth over five hundred thousand dollars because of all the splits over the years. And I saw some Ford stock, and I'm pretty sure there was at least one more big name in that pile. And what a coincidence that you found them here in our house. Who would have guessed?"

Sharon decided it was time to tell Bill about the ghost. "Bill?" she said. Just as she started to talk, the oven door fell open, and the timer went off. Bill rushed over with an oven mitt to retrieve the rest of their dinner.

Her grandfather appeared next to Bill, shaking his finger in a no-no gesture to Sharon.

Why not? Mouthed Sharon to the spirit. The spirit came to her and whispered, "You don't want people to think you're crazy, do you?"

"I think we need a new stove," said Bill. "I've never seen a door just fall open like that, but that could be a hazard. You were saying?" he said as he served up their dinner.

Sharon smiled and said, "Nothing, really. I've forgotten now. Let's just eat."

The End...

Story 11

The Trains

The sound of the train horns was making her crazy. Sometimes, they would come through three or four times per hour. The horns were so loud she could not hear her own thoughts, only the sound of the dog howling in anguish as they passed. Then, when the horns stopped, there was the vibration of the cars themselves. She could feel them vibrating over the tracks. She would hold her hands over her ears and shake herself, trying to get them to stop. It was all she could do to not join the dog in his incessant howling. Screaming would not stop the feeling or the sound, but she imagined that it would somehow make things better.

Finally, the train passed. Kim took a sip of wine and wondered why she stayed here. This dreary town with its constant train activity and nothing much else to occupy someone who was accustomed to theater and dance and museums.

"Why do I stay here?" she asked the cat.

Her husband was due to be home at any moment, but he was probably sitting on the other side of the train track. Dinner was already in the oven and would be ready when he arrived. He liked to cook when his business allowed, but today was not that day. He had been delayed by an emergency with an oil derrick in the next county. Kim had been happy to put a casserole on for the two of them.

"Honey? I'm ho-ome," he called melodically. It was a joke between the two of them, and they both still laughed at it.

"I'm in the kitchen," she called.

Bob walked in and gave her a long kiss. She snuggled up and breathed in his energy like she had been starving for it all day. She missed him when they were apart, even for a workday.

"You're the only reason I stay in this godforsaken excuse for a city, you know." She said it out loud, and it felt good.

"So, it's all my fault, eh?" he replied.

"Yes! Yes, it is," she said, almost whining. "How much longer do you think it will take to get this thing up and running?"

"Maybe another year or two," he said. "I kind of like it here. The slow pace is refreshing. Everything is so relaxed. People are so easy going."

"That's because they're so bored. These people get excited over a dead chicken! I can't relate to anyone here."

A train interrupted the conversation, and by the time it passed, she had lost her train of thought. Bob blew it off as Kim joking. He didn't realize how close she was to breaking. He still traveled with his business, spending many nights in Dallas or Atlanta or Orlando. But it was always for business, and she rarely went along. The trips were so short, it wasn't worth going.

"Let me go clean up before dinner?" Bob asked as if he needed permission.

Kim nodded. Bob kissed her on the cheek and left the room. Kim looked at the knife she had been using earlier. It was still in the sink. How easy it would be to just slit her wrists. She picked up the potential instrument of death and laid it across her wrist. She tilted it from side to side and pictured the blood spurting from her vein. Sweet release, she thought.

"Does something need slicing?" said Bob as he caressed her hands from behind. "I can help."

"No, no," she said. "I was just about to clear the sink. If you're ready, we can eat now."

"Absolutely," said Bob cheerfully. "I'll get the plates. Are we eating in the kitchen?"

"Yes," said Kim. "That will be fine. I'll get the silverware."

Kim had removed the casserole from the oven when Bob first came in. It was cooled down enough now to serve. She had already made them both a salad.

There was silence for a few minutes while they enjoyed the meal. Another train horn pierced the atmosphere, and Kim jumped.

"I don't know how much more of this I can take," she screamed. The train passed through the next two crossings with horns blaring then faded off.

Bob smiled at her. "I love you, K Bear. Why don't you go spend a few days in Dallas? You can stay at the Four Seasons in Las Colinas. Have a couple of friends stay with you. Do the Spa package and really pamper yourself? Go downtown and see a show. Doesn't that sound good?"

"I love you, too, Bob. But you really don't understand. I can do that, but then I have to come back here, back to this project of a house, back to this one-horse town…"

"Back to me," he interrupted her.

"It's not you," she said. "I love coming back to you. I love being with you. I just don't like being **here**… especially when you're away."

"I'm not going to lie, Kim. It's going to take at minimum a year and probably two years to get this company ready to market. And the real estate market in this town is," he paused, looking for the right word, "soft. I could put this house on the market today, and it would probably take a year to sell. What can I do?"

"I don't know," said Kim. "Just forget I said anything. Maybe I will go into the Four Seasons. Rachel would come and stay with me. That would be a fun getaway. I'll plan it for next week."

"That's the spirit," said Bob. "Let's find a movie to watch, maybe a romantic comedy."

Kim wasn't in the mood for a movie, but she agreed. Bob really didn't understand how she was feeling. No one did. She did not have one friend in this town, not one person she could call to go see a show or grab some lunch. She felt pathetic, and she hated the feeling.

"When is your next weekend off?" Kim asked as she joined Bob on the love seat. Bob's days off rarely fell on the traditional Saturday and Sunday. His schedule revolved around some very erratic patterns dealing with the oil wells in this region.

"Next Wednesday and Thursday," he said, "unless something changes."

"Then I'll go on into Las Colinas in a couple of days," Kim said. "I can time it so that you can join me Wednesday and Thursday. We can catch an evening show of the Phantom of the Opera. I've heard it's an excellent production with full multi-media effects."

"That sounds wonderful, Kim. Tell me where to be and when to be there."

"I'll see if Rachel wants to go with us," said Kim. "So, I can have the tickets left at "will call." I haven't been to a live production in ages. This will be fun."

Kim felt her spirits lifting the more she thought about her escape. She should have thought of this herself. Just then, the train horn blasted, and her mood deflated instantly. "Any escape is only temporary," she said after the horn stopped. "In the end, I come back to the trains."

"Hang in for another year or two," said Bob. "I'll try to make it go as quickly as possible."

The train horns sounded at least once or twice an hour for the rest of the night. At one a.m. Kim took a sleeping pill. Some nights it was the only way she managed to get any sleep at all. Everyone had told her she would get used to it. So far, everyone had been wrong.

When Kim opened her eyes in the morning, it was with hesitation and reluctance. Sleeping pills always left her a little drowsy the next day. She rubbed her eyes and looked for Bob. He seemed to be gone. He must have realized she had a rough night and left her to sleep in. She looked at the clock. Her eyes widened as it dawned on her that it was already ten a.m. How had she slept so late? She threw off her covers and started to make a mad morning dash. Then she stopped. She wasn't in Dallas today. There was no need to be in a rush.

She took her time making the bed and getting ready for the day. That sleeping pill had really knocked her out. She hadn't heard any trains, and she hadn't heard Bob leave. She felt genuinely rested for the first time in days. Kim hated taking the sleeping pills because they made her feel "not fully there" the next day, but maybe it was worth it. The train horn sounded, and she experienced it all the way up her spine. Who had invented this torture? What was karma punishing her for?

Kim heard a radio upstairs. Was Bob still home? That wouldn't be like him at all. Walking to the bottom of the staircase, she called out to him. He didn't answer. *Maybe the music is too loud for him to hear me*, she thought. She took a few steps upwards and called out to him again. There was no response. She went to the top of the stairs and looked around. There was no one in sight and the music had stopped. Were the sleeping pills affecting her hearing?

She went back downstairs just in time to receive a text from one of her clients. Could she meet them in Lewisville this afternoon at two? She moaned a little but texted back that she could.

Great! She thought. *There goes my whole afternoon. I'll be on the road for three hours or more.*

She poured a cup of coffee and nibbled on a piece of banana nut bread. *I guess that's brunch,* she thought.

The radio upstairs started again. The music seemed to be from the forties or fifties. It might have been Big Band. Kim didn't bother to call out to Bob this time. She knew he wasn't home, and crept quietly to the bottom of the steps. Taking each step slowly and deliberately being careful not to make a sound. She was on the third step from the top when the music stopped. She eased back down a few steps and waited. Minutes passed, then the music started again. It was still Big Band, but it was a different tune this time. She moved slowly up the steps. The music stopped again when she made it to the third step from the top.

As she was intent on listening, the train horn blasted, and she jumped an entire step. Her heart was now racing, and any fogginess from the sleeping pill was gone. If she could go out there and give that engineer a few healthy bumps to the head, she would surely do it right now.

She went back to the kitchen, cleared the breakfast bar, and rinsed her coffee cup. She went into her office to do a little paperwork before leaving for Lewisville. She remembered a nice restaurant with French cuisine near the office she was going to be visiting this afternoon. She would pick up a couple of meals and bring them home to reheat for tonight. She texted this information to Bob. She loved French pastry, and this little treat would make the trip to Lewisville worthwhile.

Bob texted back that he would be working very late tonight. He suggested that she enjoy a meal at the restaurant. He would grab something from a burger joint. She agreed but made a mental note to bring him a Brioche for a late-night snack.

The music started up again. Kim closed her laptop and walked to the door. Once again, the music drifted down the staircase. Back Kim walked ever so quietly up the stairs. She stopped before she reached the third step. She listened for voices. It had sounded like there was a conversation going on. She was hoping that getting this close would enable her to hear what was being said, but the conversation seemed to have stopped. Only the music remained. Once again, the train interrupted her, and again, her heart skipped a few beats. This was unnerving. When the train was past, the music had stopped. She decided to head on into Lewisville.

The meeting was pleasant, and she enjoyed the French food and atmosphere for dinner. She ordered a Brioche to go for Bob and picked out a couple of breakfast pastries, too. The drive home was riddled with traffic jams and road construction, which turned a one-and-a-half-hour trip into a two-hour journey. It was almost a relief to be home.

Kim walked into the house and took the goodies to the kitchen. She didn't bother putting them in the fridge as they would be eaten soon enough. Once again, there was music coming from upstairs. She had always enjoyed her music at the sound level of "from the next room," so it was pleasant in a way. So long as she didn't think about the fact that there was no radio up there. She had long suspected that there was a spirit in this house. At least it liked music.

She moved to the bottom of the stairs. She stood there listening, wanting to go upstairs and introduce herself, but reluctant to verify her suspicions. She knew that people would think her crazy. She already felt a bit crazy but tiptoed up the stairs without stopping at the third step. She went on up and sat down in a chair by the pool table. The upstairs was not finished yet, but Bill had gotten anxious and set up the pool table.

"Hello," she said softly. "I've been enjoying your music. I wonder why you turn it off when I come up. Are you afraid of me?" There was no response. Had she really thought there would be? Maybe she **was** going crazy; Sitting in an unfinished room talking to imaginary ghosts.

The train horn blasted her back into the present. Her whole body tensed from the sound. Her hands gripped the arms of the chair, and her teeth clenched tight. Tears rolled down her cheeks as the emotions finally overwhelmed her. She sat there crying until long after the train had passed.

"If you are real, I need to know," she said through her tears. "I mean you no harm. I just need to know that you are not some mental condition that I should see a doctor about." Kim was pleading with the spirit now. "Please play music again while I am here in the room."

Suddenly there was music. The song playing was an instrumental rendition of "At Last." Kim listened to find the source. It seemed to be coming from the other side of the room, where there were some construction tools and supplies. She walked over to it and found an old radio. It was like a boom box out of the 'Eighties. It didn't seem right for such vintage music to be coming from a more modern device. She picked up the boom box and the music stopped. She quickly put it back down.

"I'm sorry," she said. "I didn't mean to interrupt. I just didn't know this was here. Please, continue."

The music continued, but now it was another instrumental that she vaguely recognized, but could not recall the name. Kim looked at the boom box and realized it was not turned on. It wasn't even plugged in. She wanted to talk with this spirit. She tried to ask it questions, but it wasn't talking. She would have to think about a way to get some answers. For now, she sat there listening to the music and dreaming of better days.

The train horn startled her from her memories, and, as usual, she jumped. The music stopped. Bob came in downstairs, "Honey, I'm Ho-ome!" he called.

"I'm upstairs," called Kim. "I'll be right down."

"What were you doing up there?" Bob asked. "You never go up there."

"I needed to find some Christmas things from the attic."

"Bit early for that, isn't it?"

"I just wanted to know where things were and what I might need to buy." *Why am I lying?* She thought

"How was your day? Did you make arrangements for The Four Seasons?" asked Bob.

"I ended up having to go to Lewisville and forgot all about it," said Kim. *Tell him*, she thought. *Tell him about the music and the radio and the spirit!*

What if he thinks I'm crazy? She thought back to herself.

He's your husband. You can trust him. He loves you. It had turned into a full-blown conversation with herself now.

"It's okay, honey. Don't look so horrified. You can make the arrangements tomorrow. Did you talk to Rachel?"

"No, I spent most of the afternoon just driving," said Kim. "Traffic between here and Lewisville is a nightmare. Everything is under construction."

"I know. That's one of the things I like about this place. Their idea of a traffic jam is waiting for a red light. I love driving up here," Bob laughed and went into the fridge for a beer.

Kim was panicking, wanting to tell Bob everything, but afraid of what he would think. She had had a mental breakdown a couple of years ago, and she didn't want him to think that was happening again. She couldn't think about going back into the hospital.

"I'm thinking of going back into counseling," she said out loud.

"Where did that come from? You forgot to make a phone call or two. It's really not that big of a deal, honey."

*I **have** to tell him,* she thought, *or I **will** go crazy.*

"Bob, something happened," she looked at him as seriously as she knew how. "Remember I asked about the radio upstairs?"

"Yes," he answered. "I can get a stereo system set up in there by Friday if that will help."

"No, Bob. That's not the problem. I have heard big band music coming from upstairs off and on for two days."

"Well, let's go up there right now and look for the radio. Maybe it's something one of the workmen left on."

"Bob, I've been up there. There is an old radio, but it isn't hooked up. I asked the spirit to make the music start last time, and it did."

"Honey, I think seeing the counselor again might be a good idea."

"You don't believe me. I knew you wouldn't believe me. I wasn't going to tell you because I knew you would think I was crazy," sobbed Kim.

"I don't think you're crazy, Sweetheart. I just think the trains and the town and the stress are taking their toll. We've been down this road before. But we know the signs, and we can be pre-emptive now. We'll get you in to see a counselor tomorrow."

Kim was still sobbing. "This is real, Bob. I swear the music is real." As she said it, the sounds of "Chattanooga Choo Choo" came drifting down the stairs.

Bob and Kim both looked at each other questioningly.

"Go pack a bag," said Bob. "We'll stay at a hotel tonight. I'll call a realtor in the morning."

The End

Story 12

Dottie

"Mom, where do you keep the honey?" yelled Jack from the kitchen.

"It's in the cupboard by the window, Jackie," She replied, though rather weakly.

Jack finished preparing her tea and joined her in the living room. She had recently taken to sleeping on the couch. Her sleeping patterns had become erratic since she started receiving chemo and she had long since given up on the idea of "bedtime". Her treatment schedule was not as bad as it could be; she only went for chemo three mornings a week with radiation after.

"How's the nausea been today, Mom?" Jack asked. He knew what she would say, but he always asked because he knew that she was having a rougher time than she let on. He wished he could be with her more, and he felt like a poor excuse for a caregiver, but work would only tolerate so much absence.

"It's fine," she said. "You really don't need to worry about me. The doctor even said that I won't need much extra help for a few more weeks. Then I'll get very weak for a while. Then I'll start getting better. I'm doing fine, Jackie, really."

"Even so, I'm going to get a nurse to start stopping in to check on you next week. She'll be coming on the days you don't have chemo and radiation. I'll still check in on you every day, but she'll be coming in to help you with whatever you need."

"I really don't need that, Jackie. I have friends who look in on me and they will keep coming."

"I know, Mom. But it will make me feel better to have a nurse looking in. Be nice to her for me and let her help you with getting in and out of the tub and whatever else you need, okay?" said Jack, fluffing her pillow and returning the TV remote to the coffee table.

"I'll be nice to her if she's nice to me." She said, and then mumbled into her teacup, "And as long as she doesn't make fun of my friends."

"You mean your imaginary friend?" said Jack.

"That's exactly what I'm talking about!" Dottie snapped, all at once excited and agitated. "I do not have imaginary friends. My friends take good care of me when you're not around and I won't have you calling them imaginary."

"Mom, you have great friends and I am nothing but grateful for them keeping you company and looking out for you when I'm not here. But there is still that one that no one has ever seen." There was a long pause as he waited for her to respond. She chose not to.

"You'd better get on to work now," said Dottie. "Thank you for taking me to therapy today. Tell your boss I said thank you to him, too."

"I always do, Mom. Do you want some more tea before I go?"

"No, this is perfect. I love you, Son."

"I love you, too, Mom."

As Jack locked the front door and walked away, he could hear the sound of the TV. Mom had turned on one of her soap operas. As he drove away, a car pulled up and a sweet looking lady climbed out of her car.

One of his mom's friends was already there to keep her company. He didn't know most of their names, but he was glad she had so many friends to see her through this.

The staff at the cancer clinic had warned him that the more ill she became the less often her friends would come around. People don't like being around anyone who seems to be dying. Going through cancer therapy is a lot like dying. The patient will get weaker and weaker until they can barely get out of bed. It has to do with the white blood cell count. They call that lowest time the "nadir".

Mom wasn't to that point yet, but he could see that she was getting weaker every day. He would be more worried if they hadn't warned him about it early on. He had made sure to let her friends know, too. He hoped that in this way they would stick it out with her.

Then there was the imaginary friend. Her name was Lucy. He laughed out loud as he thought about her. Mom was adamant that she was real. She came around late at night when Dottie couldn't sleep. She would make tea and they would sit and talk. They talked about Dottie's antics when she was in her twenties and what it was like to be a mother and what it was like to dance all night. Lucy always steered Dottie to remembering happy times and good adventures. This lifted Dottie's spirits and seemed to increase her energy if only for a little bit.

Dottie seemed to appreciate Lucy more than anyone else. But Jack knew that none of his mom's other friends would be out that late and none of them had ever met Lucy. She wasn't from Church or the Ladies Club or the Hospital Volunteers. She didn't play Bingo with Dottie or go to the craft club. Dottie claimed she was just a neighbor friend.

But she made his mother happy, so he let it be.

Unfortunately, as the weeks went on, Jack discovered the staff had been right. The sicker Dottie got, the less her friends stopped by. Some said that she needed her rest as she was always sleeping when they came by. Some gave no reason at all –they just stopped coming by.

The Millers stepped up and offered to take her to her chemo at least once and sometimes twice a week. They were retired and had plenty of time. They had known Dottie since before her husband died. They had always been available to help when she needed things done around the house or if her car was acting up. They were the best kind of friends.

She was getting so weak that walking was an effort and they needed to use a wheelchair to get her to the car. There was a wheelchair at the cancer facility, though, so at least they didn't have to bring the wheelchair with them. They would always get her lunch after the treatment and she would usually sleep away the rest of that afternoon.

Jack would swing by after work and see that she had dinner. She wouldn't eat much because it didn't always stay down. Then they would sit and talk about Jack's day and his mother would nod off on the sofa. He was worried about her, but there was little more that he could do.

Little by little, he started noticing things that didn't add up. For example, there was the mystery of the blanket. It was one of those blankets that you pick up at Christmas, the ones with a scene. This one had an Indian princess. It was pretty and suited his mother.

"Mom, where did this blanket come from?" Jack asked.

"Lucy brought it," she said nonchalantly. "I was feeling chilled and she said it would be perfect, and it was. Not too heavy, but warm nonetheless."

"Mom, Lucy still comes by at night?" he asked with a hint of disbelief.

"Oh, yes. Sometimes she comes during the day, too."

"I'd like to meet her sometime."

"I'd like for you to meet her, too, Jackie. She's been so helpful these last few weeks."

Jack began to wonder if maybe Lucy was actually real. After all, the blanket in his hands was a very real blanket. And his mom seemed convinced that Lucy had brought it. Yes, maybe she did come by when needed. It was a comforting thought. It made him feel better about not being able to be with her all the time.

But still, there was a nagging doubt, the same uncertainty you feel when your truck finally turns over after you've been trying to start it for ten minutes. Sure, it's started, but will it stay that way? And will it start again after you shut it off? He didn't bring it back up that day.

He would come in some days to find the day's dishes drying in the sink and scold his mom for not leaving them for him.

"Oh, I didn't do them, Jackie," she would always protest. "Lucy must have done that while I was napping."

Soon the nurse he had hired began. She came in on Tuesdays and Thursdays. Tina was friendly, and Dottie appreciated that. She was much younger than most of the people Dottie saw these days and it showed in her makeup and punk hairstyle. Dottie didn't like the tattoos at first, but as she got to know Tina, she didn't mind them at all.

Tina helped Dottie bathe and picked up a bit. She made sure that all the meds were correct and saw to it that Dottie ate while she was there. This gave Jack a sense that he was doing everything he could for her. A nurse was much better qualified than Jack to spot if something was wrong or needed attention.

When Dottie had reached the nadir of the treatment and was at her absolute lowest, Jack arranged for Tina to be there every day for a week. The doctors said that she should start feeling better by then.

Through it all, she continued to talk about Lucy. Lucy, Mom said, was reading her a book from Dottie's family library that Dottie had never read before. It was a fascinating book about the history of the very city they lived in. Dottie had never known the town was so rich in historical stories. In fact, she told Jack excitedly, the house she was living in had been used as a hospital for a brief period when there had been a flu epidemic. Lucy told her that. It wasn't in the book. Lucy had done some research at the museum.

Lucy, who Jack was rapidly forgetting might be imaginary, had certainly been there for his mom through the whole grizzly ride so far. Jack felt that she had taken a great burden from him. Not that his mother was a burden, of course, but it wasn't easy taking care of her every day and holding down a job, too. And he needed his job to pay Dottie's hospital bills.

After the nadir, Lisa started coming only four days at a time. Then down to three days, and finally back to just Tuesdays and Thursdays. Dottie was not feeling great, but she was certainly feeling better. As she felt good enough to go to church again, some of her friends started coming around again. She was happy to see them and didn't seem aware that they had pretty much abandoned her during her worst times. She was just happy to see them again

After the chemo and radiation had ended, Dottie felt better and better each day. As she grew stronger, her friends didn't feel the need to come around as often. She was able to get out and visit them, instead. Life fell back into a more normal routine. The worst of the cancer saga was behind them and they started moving on. The horror had passed and they could move on.

Jack still stopped by to check on her every day, but the nurse was let go and Dottie was back to volunteering at the hospital and going to the ladies' club, and she even took up Bingo again. She wasn't home much during the day. Jack slipped back into letting her take care of herself after a while.

One day he came by after work. The days were getting longer when something odd happened. As he approached the house after work, he thought he heard the TV, but then realized it was his mother arguing with someone on the phone. She was shouting—actually shouting—which she hadn't done for years. He rushed in to see what was wrong. She stopped mid-sentence when she saw him, but there was no phone in her hand. She was standing in the kitchen, both hands raised as though she was making a very specific point.

"Mom, who are you arguing with?" he asked, confusion replacing his fear.

"Lucy!" She said, clearly frustrated.

"I finally get to meet Lucy?" he said with a smile, and crossed the living room quickly.

"She left when you came in." said his mom, and sat down in one of her wooden chairs. "She took off out the back door."

"What were you arguing about?" asked Jack, surreptitiously leaning to look out the window in a vain attempt to see Lucy walking away.

"Lucy wanted me to stay home tonight. She said I'm not as well as I think I am and that I need to slow down some." Her tone was annoyed, as if she could see the wisdom in the words but was trying her best not to, "She thinks I'm going to make myself sick again."

"Well, Mom, where were you going to go? Don't you usually stay in in the evening?" asked Jack.

"Don't you start on me, too!" cried Dottie. "I'm feeling fine and I want to go to Bingo tonight. I'll be fine. I'm not getting sick again, I'm doing much better."

"What did your doctor say last time?" asked Jack.

"He said to take it slow. He said to go at my own pace and listen to my body." She answered softly. "But Lucy thinks I need to stay in tonight."

"Tell you what. I'll take you to Bingo and if you get to feeling too tired, I'll be there to bring you home," offered Jack.

Mom shook her head, "I would hate to bother you," she said.

"No bother at all," he said. "We haven't been spending enough time together since you started feeling so much better. Let me run home and change and I'll be right back."

Jack made it back quickly enough and they went to Bingo together. Lucy had been right, too. Dottie was worn out after only two rounds and she was ready to be home. Jack helped her to the car.

"You do this all the time, you know." He chastised, "You have a good day and overdo it. You're probably going to regret it tomorrow."

"I'm regretting it a little already," she sighed. "I really thought it would be okay."

When they reached the house, there was a light on in the kitchen. Jack made a mental note to check next time they went out to make sure all the lights were out.

They went inside and Jack was surprised to find the couch "bed" made up and looking fresh, which was not how they had left it. His mother didn't seem at all surprised.

"Looks like Lucy has been here," she told him when he asked about it. "She comes by in the evenings a lot."

"Well, now I really want to meet her," said Jack.

He walked in toward the kitchen and realized the light he had seen from the street was now out. Lucy must have been there when they had pulled up and then left as they entered. The dishes were drying in the rack. Jack was forced to admit that Lucy was not only obviously real, but also that she seemed to care for his mother very much. So why did he still have this nagging feeling about her? Something just didn't feel right. It was as if the universe was teasing him, and he was in no mood for teasing these days.

Jack walked back into the living room to find that his mother was already asleep. She hadn't even bothered to change into her night clothes. She would probably be awake again in a couple of hours; she could change into PJs then. He left her a note and let himself out. He drove home with mixed emotions about her volunteer caregiver. It didn't feel right, never having met somebody she was so close to, but it was nice to know that she had help around if she needed it.

The next morning Jack woke up early so he could stop by and see how his mom was doing before work. She had clearly overdone last night and he wanted to make sure she would be okay today. When he arrived, she was already up and dressed.

"I'll probably wait a few days before I try that again," she told him. "I enjoyed the first round, but I should have listened to Lucy and stayed in. I'm very tired today."

"Next time you want to go out at night, call me," said Jack. "I will take you to dinner and then go with you to Bingo if you like. After you get your strength back, of course."

"I will, Jackie. Maybe next week would be better."

"What are you doing today?" asked Jack.

"I'm volunteering at the hospital this morning. I think I'll take this afternoon off. I'm sure I'll need the rest by then," she said.

"Let me know if you need me to come get you," he whispered as he leaned in to kiss her on the cheek. She seemed so frail at that moment.

Jack left for work and Dottie left for the hospital. She didn't tell Jack that Lucy had asked her not to go this morning. Lucy was so concerned about Dottie's health. She thought that Dottie was overdoing everything and needed to take more time to recuperate. Dottie didn't think her son needed to hear about that.

If she had mentioned it, Jack might not have felt like something in his brain had exploded when he received a phone call at work that his mother was being admitted to the hospital. It was quite lucky, the nurses said, that she was there as a volunteer. She had passed out and the ER doctor had decided to admit her for observation given her recent history. Dottie's family doctor came in later and ordered a couple of tests.

When the Oncologist came back the next morning, he had bad news. The tests showed that she would need more chemotherapy. They had really hoped the one round would take care of it, but, well, they would be in later to schedule the next round.

Jack took it harder than his mother did. Dottie had learned to go with the flow, but Jack still wanted some routines. He had become comfortable with the current routine and didn't want to have to change it so soon. Dottie didn't mind being in the hospital –she knew a lot of people there and they always took good care of her-- but she was ready to go home.

The doctor said they needed to continue monitoring her white blood cell count. It needed to get a little higher before they could begin the second round of chemo. She was almost there, but they wanted to keep her for a couple more days.

"Mom, has Lucy visited you while you've been here?" Jack asked.

"Once," answered Dottie wistfully. "She came in on the first night and said the bright lights in the hallways hurt her eyes. She said it made her uncomfortable and I really didn't need her here with all these people to help. I miss her company, though."

"Maybe you could call her and ask her to come visit again since you're going to be here longer than you thought."

"She'll come by if she can," Dottie said with a smile, and he pursued it no further.

Two days later, Jack brought Dottie home. She was scheduled to begin chemo again on Monday. She would go Monday, Wed, and Friday, but this time there would be no radiation. Jack wasn't looking forward to seeing his mother suffer again. He hoped that her friends would be able to visit and help as much as they had last time, but he had his doubts.

The house was clean and the sofa was ready for her when they walked in and Dottie went straight to it. Jack made sure she had all the meds she needed and left for work. It was mid-morning. She would have a few more days to recuperate before the next round of chemo started. Maybe he would take her out to a movie this weekend. She would enjoy that. And hopefully Lucy would come over for a visit. He knew his mom was missing her.

The days passed quickly and Dottie went to Bingo and the movies and tried to squeeze in as much as possible while she was feeling better. She knew the routine now and knew that it was only a matter of weeks before she would not feel like even walking to the door. Jack took her to the movies several times and several of her friends visited with her in the afternoons.

The same couple that had taken her to chemo during the first round volunteered to take her twice a week this time. Jack appreciated the help since he really needed to be at work as much as possible. He told them how grateful he was for their help and they were more than happy to do it and spend the time with Dottie.

Lucy came by in the evenings when no one was around and read to Dottie from several books that Dottie had never read before.

Dottie started slowing down after the first week and by the third week she was not as chipper as she had been the first time around. There was something different now. Lucy made her chicken soup and sometimes Dottie was so weak that Lucy had to help her get the spoon to her mouth.

Then the coughing started. Fits of deep, wet coughs that lasted for minutes. The doctor at the chemo center told her not to be around any smokers. She told him she wasn't. She stayed at home most of the time.

"Jack, will you talk to the doctor for me this morning? I feel so congested and all he says is that

I need to stay away from smokers." She said before the Wednesday morning check-up and treatment.

"I'll go in there with you and see what he says." He doubted that the doctor had actually said that; after all she didn't have any smoker friends. He was sure she had misheard or misremembered, and was quite confused later in the exam room.

"Doctor, my mother seems very sick. She never was this sick the first go round."

"She is just reacting to the smoke," the doctor said, as though it were obvious.

"What smoke? I don't smoke. She doesn't smoke," said Jack.

"I can smell the smoke on her and her friends when they come in on Monday and Friday," he said. "They need to stop smoking around her."

"They don't smoke around me," said Dottie, mildly offended. "I explained to them how harmful that would be."

"Doctor, you really need to check her out again," said Jack, who was more interested in a definitive answer than this go-nowhere argument.

The doctor listened to her chest again and said, "Let's get an x-ray and see what we're dealing with."

Dottie was taken back for an x-ray while Jack waited. An hour later the nurse called him into a treatment room. The doctor came in and told him that they were going to admit her; she had pneumonia. They would be giving her IV antibiotics for a couple of days and then she would be able to go home. They would do the Friday chemo in the hospital.

One of Dottie's "hospital volunteer friends" came in and told Jack she would stay with Dottie through admitting and see her to her room. Jack thanked her and headed to his mom's house to get her hospital bag. On the drive, he grew more than a little concerned. What kind of dog and pony show were they running up there if they could let a little old lady suffer with pneumonia for two days without diagnosing it?

What else were they missing? He thought.

When he arrived at the house, he saw someone looking out the living room window. A round face and dark hair that disappeared almost instantly. It had to be Lucy. He was going to meet the woman this time. He ran into the house, through the empty living room, and headed immediately toward the back door. And yet there was no one in the house and no one in the back yard.

307

He really wanted to talk to her, wanted to tell her that his mom wasn't doing well and would be gone for a few days. He went out the back door and followed the overgrown wooden fence around the house to the gate. There was no sign of her. He walked through the back side gate to see if she had gone down the side street. He saw the backdoor neighbor out watering his garden.

"Did you see Lucy come by here a minute ago?" Jack asked the neighbor.

"Who's Lucy?" he responded.

"She's a friend of my mom," said Jack.

"And who's your mom?" said the neighbor.

"I'm sorry, my name is Jack. I'm Dottie's son. She lives here in this house."

"Dottie?" He sounded pleasantly surprised, "Why didn't you say so? Such a nice lady. Don't know any Lucy, though."

"She's been coming over to see my mom a lot. Mom said she was a neighbor and she uses the back door most of the time." The neighbor looked askance at him.

"Son, look at the flowers grown up around that gate. It hasn't been used in a long time."

Jack looked at the gate he had just come through. There were vines and stems on a couple of plants, all broken by his recent exit. Sure enough, it had not been used recently.

"Well," Jack said, losing steam, "I guess I'll have to ask my mom about where Lucy lives."

"You do that. How's your mom doing, by the way? We were sure sorry to hear about the cancer."

"She was getting better, but she took a turn for the worse today and they put her in the hospital. They say she'll be there for a few days."

"Well, you tell her Tom and Betty send their best."

"Thank you. I will," said Jack, and left frustrated.

He called on a couple of other neighbors to let them know about his mom and to see if they knew where Lucy lived. No one had heard of her. One of the ladies told him that she had been bringing casseroles over for his mom once a week, and hadn't seen anyone. He thanked her and went on back to the house to get his mom's things.

Jack grabbed his mom's bag and went back to the hospital. She was in her own room now. He walked in as she and her friend were laughing about something. "Mom, I have your bag here. I hope it has everything you need," said Jack.

"I'm sure it does. I won't need much," she said with a smile.

"Mom, I ran into your neighbor, Tom. I asked him where Lucy lived so I could let her know how you are doing. He said he didn't know of anyone named Lucy."

"I bet he just forgot her," Dottie declared. "He's not as sharp as he once was. Betty probably knows Lucy. But you know, I'm not even sure where Lucy lives. In fact, I never knew her before I got sick."

"Really? She just showed up one day?" asked Jack with a little bit of attitude.

"Yes." She replied, with a hint of her old scolding-mother voice, "She came to the back door. She was so nice. She offered to sit with me while I waited for you to give me a ride to that first Dr.'s appointment. I remember I was so nervous and she calmed me down."

The nurse came in to give Dottie a breathing treatment and asked Jack to wait outside. He realized that he hadn't eaten yet, so he went downstairs to get a snack.

As he ate, he thought about how none of this business with Lucy made any sense. He had never met Lucy, but he had seen plenty of evidence that she was visiting his mom regularly, that she was a real person. So how had the neighbors never heard of her? What was he missing?

When he walked back in to his mother's room she was exhausted from the breathing treatment. She could barely keep her eyes open to talk. He kissed her and told her he would see her in the morning.

His thoughts were everywhere on the drive home. He almost felt dizzy from it and more than a little crazy. He was trying to fit a square peg into a round hole to make sense of all the information (and lack of information). He would ask around the neighborhood on Saturday. Or was the neighborhood trying to play some cruel joke on him? Were they all in on it? Did they all know who Lucy was and were just choosing not to tell him? Was he going mad or just paranoid? What did they have to gain from not telling him about her?

He drove to the hospital on his lunch and found Mom in the middle of pretending to eat her food. It wasn't much of a lunch to begin with, but it didn't look like she had touched it. He hadn't noticed until that moment how thin and frail she had become. She hadn't been eating well and hadn't been keeping much down. He winced at the thought of losing her to so mundane a thing as pneumonia after winning for so long against cancer.

"How are you feeling today, Mom?" he asked quietly.

"It hurts when I cough, but I think it might be getting better," she answered.

"Have you had any friends come to visit yet?"

"Just the ones that work here, but that is a lot," she said.

"Lucy didn't stop in?" he asked.

"No, but I wasn't expecting her to," she said.

"I'd like to call and offer her a ride if she wants to visit," said Jack hoping to get an idea of where to look for her.

"She'll come if she feels the need, don't you worry about it. Why don't you eat my lunch, Jackie? I don't want it." Dottie had tried, to no avail, to push the food off on someone else several times. But the nurses kept track of how much she ate. They were talking about having to place a feeding tube.

"No, Mom, that's yours and you need to eat at least some of it."

"That's exactly right," said the nurse as she entered. She turned to Jack and quietly added, "Can I talk to you for a moment outside?"

They walked out into the hall, and she said rather abruptly, "Did I hear you talking about a friend named Lucy?"

"Yes, it's a friend of my mom's and I've never met her. Will you let me know if she comes to visit?"

"I don't think you will be meeting Lucy anytime soon," she said shaking her head. "Lucy visits a lot of our patients, but no one other than a patient has ever seen her. Most of us think she is a figment of their imagination. You know one patient tells the next one and they all believe in her. She comes to keep company with the sick and dying."

"My mother isn't dying," snarled Jack. "She has pneumonia, but she will be over it soon and then she will be home again." Jack wasn't liking the sound of this. He knew Lucy was real. She had fixed his mom tea. She had straightened the living room while he and his mom were at Bingo. She had to be real.

"Are you saying that they imagine her or that she's a ghost?" he asked quietly. "I never said the word ghost," protested the nurse. "But it does seem odd that they all seem to have the same imaginary friend. Doesn't it?"

"You expect me to believe that Mom is being visited and helped by a GHOST? Is everyone here crazy? First the Doctor doesn't discover that she has pneumonia because he thinks she's smoking, which she doesn't. Now, you expect me to believe that there's a ghost who visits all the dying patients?"

"I didn't say she was a ghost. I think she's just imaginary. They just all seem to imagine the same person," offered the nurse trying to calm Jack down.

"You think my mother is dying, though, don't you? You said she visits the dying."

"They don't always die," she tried to soothe him.

"Maybe if I bring in a different doctor, they will be able to cure this pneumonia. That's what she's fighting now, after all."

"Everything that can be done is being done. There is no other treatment for this. And if believing in an imaginary ghost makes her feel better, then that might be what gets her through it."

"So, there is hope. She could recover. And this ghost could help."

Jack went back to his mother's room. "Mom, I have to get back to work. I'll stop in later tonight. Okay?" Too late he saw that she had dozed off. He backed out of the room like a child who had been caught trying to watch TV from the doorway after bedtime. He left the hospital and went back to work.

Work passed as slowly as waiting for a package from the Sears catalog. Jack was there in body, but not in spirit. He needed to find out what was wrong with his mother. He wanted to find out more about Lucy, or whoever it was that had been coming into his mother's home and tidying up and keeping her company and reading to her. He needed to find Lucy so that maybe she could help his mother recover. As soon as work was done, he went to her house.

The house looked freshly cleaned, but the sofa was back to being a sofa. All the dishes were put away, and there was nothing drying in the rack. It didn't look like a "sick" house at all. Maybe someone from the church had stopped by and straightened the place.

When he arrived at the hospital, his mother was not in her room, so he went to the nurse's station to ask about her.

"I'm sorry." Said the night nurse, "She's been moved to Critical Care Unit. You'll need to move her things out of the room. If you'll take them out to the car and come back, I'll show you where she is,"

Jack did as he was instructed. He had a lot of questions, and he sorted them out in his head as he transported her clothes and books. He waited patiently as the nurse finished what she was doing and she led him to the elevator. "Go to the third floor and look for the signs that say CCU. Your mother is in bed five."

Jack stood at the elevator, his eyes vacant and his arms hanging limply by his sides. He felt like a bottle being tossed about on the water. He had only been gone for a few hours. What had happened?

He followed the nurse's directions and presently came to the CCU desk. The nurse there was abrupt; his mother could not have visitors right now.

"But, I'm her son. I need to find out what's going on!" he cried.

This new nurse took him aside and led him through a door with more annoyance than pity. From where they stood, he could see every bed. They were in what looked like cubicles, in a semi-circle around the nurse's station. There were seven beds and three nurses- monitoring the beds, both visually and on screens that showed all kinds of numbers. Some of the patients had Oxygen masks on. His mother did not.

"What is going on?" he whispered.

"You don't have to whisper." She said, "Most of these patients are only barely aware that they are here. They are all in critical condition."

"Why didn't someone call me?" he whispered still.

"There was nothing you could have done. Your mother is critical, but stable for now. The pneumonia had gotten quite a foothold with her and we had to do an emergency tracheostomy to clear her airways. We are keeping her on oxygen and high doses of antibiotics right now. She won't be going for chemo tomorrow. The doctor will probably suspend chemo for now. She only had two more sessions to go and they would only be detrimental to her health at this point."

He felt light headed and dizzy. Surely this was some strange nightmare and he would wake up any minute, he told himself. The nurse led him back to his mother with a firm hand. She let him sit with her for a few minutes. He had tears spilling from his eyes as he saw his mother in such a helpless state. He didn't know what to do. Surely, he should do something, shouldn't he? He walked to the nurse's station. His mother's nurse stopped to talk with him.

"You have questions," she said.

"I do." He said, and he let the flood gates open, "How long will this take? Will she go home from here or back to another hospital room? Is she in a coma or sleeping or, what? Will she know I'm here if I stay? When can I be in the room with her? Are there specific visiting hours?"

"Whoa. Let's take this one step at a time. Your mother's lungs became so filled that we had to do an emergency tracheostomy. She's now breathing through a hole in her chest. She will be here until her condition is no longer considered critical. She is not in a coma, but she is receiving a lot of pain meds and she will be sleeping most of the time. She can only have immediate family to visit and that is limited to two at a time. It's best to come around meal time, even though your mother won't be eating. The Doctor will want to talk to you about putting in a feeding tube."

"Will she get better?"

"Her oxygen levels are low and that is what we're fighting now. But she is stable and that is a good sign. There is nothing you can do here, so go get some rest. Do what you need to do. I have your number, and we'll call you if things change."

"How did this happen so fast? I was just here at lunch and she seemed fine."

"Your mother's system is weak because of the chemotherapy. This pneumonia is very aggressive. It moves quickly. Go home. Get some food and some rest."

Friday was like a horrid dream. He didn't remember getting up or going to work, even though he was on a job when the call came. At around noon, "You need to come to the hospital as soon as possible."

He fought through the confusion and light headedness and disbelief and went to the hospital. His mother's oxygen had dropped too low. They were doing everything they could, but it continued to drop. He sat with her, watching the numbers drop. She was sleeping. There was so much he wanted to say to her. He told her how much he loved her, of course. Then he told her about the house being ready for her to come home. He told her that he had met someone that knew Lucy. He had questions that he wanted to ask, but she would not be able to respond.

At Five-o-three she stopped breathing. The nurse came in and ushered him out so they could make the body more presentable. At five-thirty, they let him back in. All the tubes were gone and she seemed to be sleeping. He didn't know what to do.

At six-thirty the nurse came in and told him he should leave. They were going to move her now. He would see her again at the funeral home.

319

Linda Anthony Hill

"Don't forget your book," called the nurse.

"I didn't bring a book."

"It was by the bed." She put a hardback book in his hands, "You've been her only visitor, so we assumed it was yours."

He stared blankly at a well-worn copy of ON DEATH AND DYING by Elizabeth Kubler-Ross. Somehow, he knew Lucy had been there.

Jack drove home in the same dreamy haze. He couldn't get his mind around the idea that his mother was gone. He wanted to pick up the phone and call her to talk about it. She would have been able to help him make sense of it. He would never be able to do that again.

The funeral was well attended. Dottie had had a lot of friends and most of them turned out for the service. She had been active in the church, so the preacher was able to talk about her as a friend. People shook Jack's hand and offered their condolences. Some even said he should come by for dinner some time. Everyone loved Dottie.

Jack was still haunted by the thought of Lucy. He knew she must be a ghost, but he didn't want to accept it. Surely, he had not left his mother in the care of a ghost all those nights. He asked the preacher if he knew Lucy, but he had never heard of her.

Jack went back to work. He was finishing up a restoration on an older home south of the courthouse. It was a beautiful old house and it had been a pleasure to be involved in restoring it to its original glory.

The owners were friends of his, Roger and Mary. They knew what had happened with his mother and they knew that he had been keeping to himself too much since her passing. They were having a "Para Party" to celebrate finishing the remodel. There would be a psychic and several ghost hunters and family and friends and they insisted that Jack come.

When he arrived it was just getting started. There was a psychic preparing to do a Gallery Reading. That meant she would be listening to ghosts and just giving out messages to each person in the room that she received a message for.

As soon as Jack sat down, she said, "You have someone with you," pointing directly at Jack. He squirmed but said nothing.

"There is a woman. No, there are two women. One is your mother and the other is," she paused and then her face lit up like she was seeing an old friend, "Lucy!" she exclaimed "It's Lucy."

"You can see her?" said Jack in disbelief.

"She's right here." The psychic said, as though explaining something to a child "She says that you have a lot of questions and I should fill you in on who she is and what she does."

"You see, Jack," She said, looking him in the eye. The other guests were dead silent, entranced by the new development, "Lucy was a nurse during the Spanish Flu pandemic that spread through the country between Nineteen-eighteen and Nineteen-twenty. She lived and worked right here in town and for a time in your mother's house. She nursed some back to health, but mostly she just made people as comfortable as possible while they died. She died herself of the Spanish Flu in Nineteen -twenty. And After spending all that time helping people die, she just kept on doing it. She visits terminally ill patients and keeps them company. She reads to them. She tries to make them comfortable."

Jack just stared at her. "She's a ghost?" he asked finally. The psychic smiled warmly.

"I prefer to call them spirits, but yes, she is from the other side. She says she left you a book to read that would help you to grieve your mother. Have you read it yet?"

"No, I haven't." Jack started to cry, from shame, grief, or embarrassment, he couldn't say.

"That's alright, dear," said the psychic. "Your mother says to read it when you can, but don't worry about it."

Jack couldn't stop crying now. His throat was tight, his nose was running; he needed to leave. He stumbled out of the house with his friend tagging right behind. "Sit here on the porch, Jack, until you feel better. Please don't try to drive like this."

He never entered his mother's house again. He donated all of its contents to the church and sold it. He wanted no reminders of the bizarre events that had taken place there. He did, however, read the book. It helped, just like she knew it would.

The End

Story 13

The OuiJa Board

They were getting the house ready for the haunted sleepover. This old place had seen better days, but it still had electricity in parts of the house, and they had put a window air conditioner in the room they were all going to actually sleep in tonight.

When her friends had heard the rumors about the place being haunted and found out that Linda and her husband were not renting it out anymore, they had begged to have a haunted sleepover. They loved ghost stories and knew this would be a blast.

Jenn had brought a digital camera, and Mandy had brought a OuiJa board and a digital voice recorder. Linda had a TV/DVR and some scary movies. Ashleigh had made cookies and brownies which were always perfect for a slumber party. Everyone brought sleeping bags and plenty of snacks. They were pretty excited.

Linda didn't really expect anything to happen, but she didn't want to disappoint her friends. They had been talking about this since she and her husband agreed to it. He had decided to stay in the bedroom downstairs while they investigated the upstairs apartment. He wanted nothing to do with ghost hunting or a haunted sleepover, but he didn't want them staying the night without someone keeping watch.

The downstairs bedroom was kind of a joke. Linda had brought in a queen-sized blow-up mattress and put it on a bed frame with plywood for the base. They found an old recliner and put in a lamp, a clock, and a window air conditioner. It was their weekend home away from home when they came to Gainesville to work on their properties.

This would be the first haunted sleepover, and they were all hoping to have something happen. It took about an hour to settle in and get the "beds" ready. There was a bathroom upstairs, but everyone was afraid to stay in it long enough to take a bath in the clawfoot tub.

They had all just rinsed off and gotten on their PJs when Mandy decided they needed to set up the OuiJa board in the upstairs sitting room. It was a glow in the dark board that she had found at a toy store. The room was not that dark as it had windows all the way around three sides. The moon wasn't full, but it wasn't new either, so there was barely enough light to see. But it was enough.

They set it up and sat down to play, but Mandy said, "No. We're going to leave it here for an hour and come back and see if the planchette has moved." Everyone agreed it was a good plan.

"What do we do while we wait?" asked Ashleigh. "Do you want to watch a movie now?"

"No," said Mandy. "We could just walk around downstairs and take some pictures first."

"I want a picture of me in that clawfoot tub," said Jenn.

They walked around looking for photo ops and then went through the camera looking for anything abnormal. They found a couple of orbs and were encouraged that it was a good sign of what was to come.

Linda had brought her Runes and offered to do Rune readings for anyone that wanted one. Ashleigh was first, and it was a strange reading.

"I haven't seen this before," said Linda. "All the Runes are upside down or backward. They also all appear to be negative." Linda tried to keep the reading as light as possible, but the Runes said what they said and it was tough to sugar coat it. Ashleigh was in for some bad times.

"Me next!" said Mandy.

Linda laid out the Runes and realized that they were almost identical to Ashleigh's casting. This was most unusual. "Mandy, I don't know how to explain this. It is almost the same as Ashleigh. Do you want me to mix them up and cast again?"

"Well," said Mandy, "maybe that would be a good idea. If you think maybe they weren't mixed up enough."

Linda shook up the bag of custom-made silver Runes and drew them out one at a time. "This just can't be," she said. "All the Runes are positive, but they are all reversed, which makes them negative. Do you even want me to read it?"

"Sure," said Mandy. "It can't be that bad. You always know how to put a positive spin on things."

Linda read the Runes and tried to make it as positive as she could. But it looked like Mandy was in for as rough a time as Ashleigh.

"Jenn, it's your turn."

"Do I look stupid?" said Jenn. "I don't need a negative reading in a haunted house. Forget it!"

"Why don't we go check the OuiJa board," said Mandy, trying to lighten things up.

They walked out to the sitting room. There was no furniture in this room, and it had old fashioned hardwood floors. The OuiJa board was glowing eerily in the center of the room.

"Has anyone been out here playing with it?" asked Mandy.

Everyone replied, "No."

"It's moved! It was in the center, and now it's on number five. Linda, it moved by itself," said Mandy. She seemed a tad concerned. "I'm going to set it back in the center and see if it moves again."

She reset the planchette, and everyone took a seat around it waiting to see it move by itself. After about five minutes, they decided that maybe they needed to leave. Perhaps it would only work if no one was watching.

"Let's go watch Joe's scary movie," said Linda. "That will kill some time."

"I don't know if I need a scary movie," said Jenn. "This is already getting scary. That bathtub was creepy, and there's no way I'm going down that creepy back staircase. There's something mean down there."

"We could watch Ghostbusters," said Linda. "That's not scary at all."

"No," said Mandy. "I really want to watch Joe's movie. I've been waiting to see it, and knowing Joe, it's probably not all that scary anyway."

"Bang!" came a noise from what seemed like the room they were going to be sleeping in. They all crept cautiously in to see what had happened. There was nothing that looked out of place.

"Maybe it was outside," said Ashleigh. "Let's go ahead and watch a movie."

"Where are the DVDs?" asked Mandy.

"They're right there on the mantle by the TV," said Linda.

"No, they're not," said Mandy. "I know they were here. I saw them. But they're gone."

"Well, they must be here somewhere," said Linda. "Everyone, just search around. Maybe we moved them before."

They searched the room. No DVDs.

"How many were there?" asked Ashleigh.

"There was a stack of at least four, maybe five," said Mandy.

"I want to go home," said Jenn. "This place is officially creeping me out."

"We can't leave yet," said Mandy. "It's just getting started."

"I don't care," said Jenn. "I need to leave, and we're in **my** car!"

"Wait! Wait!" yelled Mandy in a whisper. "Let me go check the OuiJa board first."

"I'm not going over there," said Jenn. "You're not getting me anywhere near those stairs again."

"I'll go with you," said Ashleigh.

Mandy and Ashleigh went to check on the board or more precisely on the planchette. They both screamed as they came running back in. "It's back on the number five! It's back on the number five!"

Jenn already had her things ready to leave. "Mandy, are you coming with me, or not?" she asked.

"Will you give me a ride back, Ashleigh? Please?" she pleaded.

"Okay," said Ashleigh.

Jennifer practically flew out the door. Linda followed her out and down the front staircase to the front door. Jenn struggled with frustration as she tried to unlock the door to open it. "Let me out!" she screamed as she pounded on the door.

Linda pushed her aside and fiddled with the door. It wasn't opening for her either.

"I want OUT!" yelled Jenn. The door flew open, almost smacking her in the head as it did.

Jenn took off out the door and straight to her car. She was in the car and down the street before Linda had the door entirely locked again.

Linda ran back upstairs to avoid being alone in this place. The girls were looking for the DVDs. Jenn had left her sleeping bag, but Linda would take it to work on Monday.

"Is everybody okay?" asked Linda.

"I think it's just a lot of coincidences," said Ashleigh.

"I think this place is way haunted," said Mandy enthusiastically. "And I hope we get a lot more activity."

"Jenn was certainly scared enough," said Linda.

"I just wish we could find those movies," said Mandy. "I really wanted to see that one."

"Y'all want to try the Ouija board in here?" asked Ashleigh.

"Sure!" said Mandy. "Maybe we can find out where the movies are."

Mandy went to get the board, and Linda cleared a place on the floor. They didn't have a table in here. Mandy set up the board and the three of them took places so that Mandy and Ashleigh could share the planchette.

"Okay, let's get serious," said Mandy. "I'm going to ask the questions. Be sure not to put any pressure on the planchette," she said to Ashleigh.

"Where are our movie discs?" she asked.

The planchette began to move instantly. G-O-N-E.

"We know that," said Mandy "Where are they gone to?" G-O-N-E

"Are you a ghost?" asked Ashleigh.

"I'm supposed to ask the questions!" said Mandy.   YES

"Did you take our movies?" asked Mandy. YES

"Will you bring them back?   NO

"Do you want us to be here?"   NO

333

"Do you want us to leave?"

The door to the kitchen slammed shut. Everyone jumped. It had startled them all, and it took a few minutes to settle back down.

"Are you a man?"   YES

"Is this your house?"   YES

"How old are you?"   G-O –H-O-M-E

The clock fell off the wall.

"I think we should go," said Ashleigh. "He obviously doesn't want us here, and he's capable of moving things. This is getting too scary! OUCH! Something just pinched my arm! I'm getting out of here!"

"Maybe that's not such a bad idea," said Mandy. "Let's pack everything up, okay?"

They packed up their things and ran down the stairs leaving Linda sitting there alone. They had left a few things, so Linda knew they were coming back for them. The OuiJa board was still there, and Mandy wouldn't go without that. It was expensive.

She sat there waiting. Then she heard the car start up and drive off. Linda was afraid of the dark when there was nothing spooky going on. She was about to be in a full panic attack. Then the planchette moved by itself.

G-O-H-O-M-E

Linda, screamed, jumped up and ran down the stairs, screaming "GOOD-BYE," only to remember that her husband was in the bedroom at the back of the house. She started screaming his name, ran back and told him they had to go.

"Where are the girls?" he asked.

"They left," she screamed. "First Jenn left and then Mandy and Ashleigh left. They just left me there all by myself, and there is something up there it took the DVDs and it told us to go home. I want out of here. Please, can we leave?" she begged.

He had heard nothing of all their adventure, but he agreed to take her home. There would be plenty more opportunities to have experiences in this house. He had already had a few himself, but this wasn't the time to tell her about them. That would keep until they were safe and sound in their real house.

He gathered up his things, and they walked to the front of the house to leave. The front door was sticking. He made a mental note to fix that next time he was in town.

The End

Hill House Manor™

Gainesville, Texas

www.HillHouseManor.com

About the Author

 Linda Anthony Hill is originally from Central Florida. She spent most of her life working in the dental laboratory industry. In fact, she retired having Mastered dental technology. Over the course of that forty-five-year career. Linda was President and CEO, for thirty-five years, of her own dental lab corporation with over fifteen employees in their hay-day.

She published her first book before retiring from dentistry and has been writing ever since. Her preferred genre is Paranormal Mystery. She even has a children's paranormal series. Her paranormal cozy mystery, THE ANCHOR IS THE KEY has won two awards for literary fiction. THE SPIDER HOUSE has won First Place for Paranormal Fiction in the Pencraft Awards for 2019.

Linda lives with her Husband, Del, in North Texas near the house that inspired these stories, Hill House Manor. You can find her other books at: amazon.com/author/hilllin She looks forward to reading your comments on this book and all her books on Amazon, as well.

Linda@HillHouseManor.com

www.HillHouseManor.com

www.amazon.com/author/hilllin

The Anchor Is The Key

The Spider House

Branden's Ghosts:

> The First Hunt

> Branden's Ghost Hunters

> The Monster Under The Bed

Sirere's Calf

The Early Years (Kindle only, but included in this book)

Non-fiction:

Hill House Manor: The Guest Book

Finding UP

Bookkeeping for Authors (Kindle only)

Made in the USA
Columbia, SC
30 October 2020